DISCARD

BAYGIRL

DISCARD

BAYGIRL

Heather Smith

ORCA BOOK PUBLISHERS

Library and Archives Canada Cataloguing in Publication

Smith, Heather, 1968-
Baygirl / Heather Smith.

Issued also in electronic formats.
ISBN 978-1-4598-0274-2

I. Title.
PS8637.M5623B39 2013   jc813'.6   C2013-901882-4

First published in the United States, 2013
Library of Congress Control Number: 2013935299

Summary: When Kit's alcoholic fisherman father loses his job,
the family is forced to leave the Newfoundland outport they call home.

*Orca Book Publishers is dedicated to preserving the environment and
has printed this book on Forest Stewardship Council® certified paper.*

Orca Book Publishers gratefully acknowledges the support for its publishing programs
provided by the following agencies: the Government of Canada through the Canada Book
Fund and the Canada Council for the Arts, and the Province of British Columbia
through the BC Arts Council and the Book Publishing Tax Credit.

Cover design by Teresa Bubela
Cover images by Getty Images and Steve Feltham
Author photo by Robin Smith

ORCA BOOK PUBLISHERS
PO Box 5626, Stn. B
Victoria, BC Canada
V8R 6S4

ORCA BOOK PUBLISHERS
PO Box 468
Custer, WA USA
98240-0468

www.orcabook.com
Printed and bound in Canada.

16 15 14 13 • 4 3 2 1

To Duncan, Rosie and April
And, always, to Rob

ONE
Tickle Cove Pond

As soon as I opened the door, I could smell it. I looked at my watch. It was only three twenty in the afternoon. But time of day never made any difference to him. He had a whiskey with his bacon and eggs once. He drank it out of a coffee mug, as if that made it okay.

I threw my backpack on the kitchen floor and put the kettle on.

"How was school today, my marvelous daughter?"

"Fine."

"What did you do?"

"We talked about *The Old Man and The Sea*."

"Ah, Hemingway."

Sounding surprised might set him off, so I kept my voice flat. "You've read it?"

He leaned back in his chair and rubbed his chin. "I certainly have, Kitty, I certainly have. Wonderful book, marvelous, just marvelous."

He looked ridiculous, trying to act intelligent.

"So what did you think of it?" he asked, pouring himself another drink.

I threw a teabag in a mug and snorted. "I thought, *Catch the marlin, old man, and put me out of my misery.*"

My father's jaw hardened. "You think it's that easy, do you? Fishin'? You think you just go out on a boat, catch a few fish and come home again?"

For a second I thought about walking away, but the idea evaporated as quickly as the wisps of steam rising from the kettle.

I leaned against the counter and folded my arms. "I never said it was easy."

"Sounds to me like you did. Sounds to me like you think it's the easiest job in the world."

"All I'm saying is that it took the old man a long time to catch one measly fish."

Dad tried to stand up but couldn't quite get his balance. He gave up, waving a finger for emphasis instead. "Measly fish?" he yelled. "Measly fish?"

The rumblings inside the kettle grew louder.

"Lemme tell you something, my lady, I've had my own struggles with the ocean and its creatures and I can really understand that Santiago fella."

Eye contact might give the impression I was interested, so I looked away. I stared at the stupidest clock ever invented, a monstrosity my father had won at darts twenty years ago. There were bottles of beer where the numbers should be, and my father never tired of announcing it was "beer o'clock" whenever anyone asked the time.

"Are you listenin' to me, Kitty?"

The whistle from the kettle was piercing, an irritating soundtrack to an irritating discussion.

"Sorry, I was just admiring the clock."

"Don't be smart with me, young lady."

"Okay, I'll be dumb with you. That way we'll be on the same intellectual level."

My father slammed his fist down on the table. "Why can't we ever have a normal conversation?"

Replies flooded my brain. *Because you're not a normal person. Because you're always drunk. Because you're an idiot.* But I knew better than to say any of them out loud, so I just shrugged.

He poured himself another drink. "What? No smart comebacks?"

I looked at his bloodshot eyes, his flushed cheeks, the broken veins on his nose. "Nope."

When my father spoke again, his voice was barely audible over the sound of the screeching kettle. "I think you owe me an apology."

I switched the stove off. "For what?"

He didn't answer right away. He just stared into his shot glass.

"Cue the dramatic pause," I muttered.

My father looked hurt. Genuinely. I pretended not to notice.

"Everything I do, Kitty, is for you. Everything. And you just throw it back in my face. Every time."

It was a classic move, the "poor me" act. I'd seen it a thousand times, and I wasn't falling for it.

"Well? What do you have to say for yourself, young lady?"

I didn't bother pouring the boiled water into my mug. I wouldn't be there to drink it.

"I'm sorry," I said.

He went from sad to smug in an instant.

"Sorry that you're such a friggin' loser."

The look on his face was priceless.

I was out the door before he'd wobbled his way to standing. And, as always, I ran to Nan's.

MY GRANDMOTHER LIVED up the road from us in a little blue house set high on a hill. I couldn't tell you much about her bedroom. Or her living room. Or any other part of her house, for that matter. But I knew every inch of her kitchen. The yellow walls, the old-fashioned stove in the corner, the rocker by the window and the ancient transistor radio on the windowsill that was rarely turned off. Nan's kitchen overlooked the whole of Parsons Bay. From her rocker I could see the church, the school and the colorful wooden homes of our neighbors and friends. The inlet, flanked by steep, rugged cliffs, was the focal point. It was a busy spot where fishing boats puttered in and out and old men long retired from the trade gathered to tell tall tales about their days out at sea. The fish plant sat not far from the wharves, where fishing nets lay drying and local boats were docked. Tangled clumps of bright-orange buoys littered the ground, waiting for their chance to bob about in the Atlantic Ocean, which, from Nan's window, looked endless.

I was five when I first escaped to Nan's.

Dad had been in his smelly old recliner that reeked of alcohol, watching *The Price is Right*. I was sitting on the floor in the kitchen, playing with pots and pans and pretending to cook like our neighbor, Ms. Bartlett, who always had something interesting in her oven. Taking inspiration from her exotic recipes, I shook imaginary spices into my pot.

"A dash of curry powder," I sang. "A pinch of fennel."

My mother, who was scrubbing the kitchen counters, shook her head and laughed. "This is Parsons Bay, Kit. Not Bombay."

A new word. Bombay. I liked it.

"Bombay!" I said. "Bombay! Bombay! Bombay!"

"For God's sake!" Dad yelled. "Get that child to shut her trap. I can't hear the Showcase Showdown."

"Showcase Showdown!" I said. "Showcase Showdown! Showcase Showdown!"

My mother put a rubber-gloved finger to her lips and whispered, "Like this, Kit. Shhhhowcase Shhhhowdown."

I tried it.

"Good girl," she said. "Now get back to your cooking. Quietly this time."

I flipped a plastic egg timer over and stirred.

"Want a taste?" I asked when the last grain of sand had fallen through the hourglass.

Mom bent over and slurped from the wooden spoon I held to her lips.

"Mmmmm. Delicious!"

"Play with me," I said.

My mother looked at the partially scrubbed counters. "I'm kind of busy…"

"I have dessert too." I tempted her with a tinfoil pie pan filled with crumpled tissues. "Lemon meringue."

She looked at the clock on the wall.

"Is it beer o'clock?" I asked.

A scowl crossed my mother's face. "No."

"What time is it then?"

The hall clock started to chime. "You tell me," she said. "Listen."

I counted the bongs. "Twelve!"

Dad must have counted too. "Where's my bloody lunch?" he yelled. "I'm bloody starving!"

My mother straightened up. "Sorry, Kit. I'll have to take a rain check on that pie."

I covered my pie pan with a tea towel. "I'll keep it warm for you."

"Good idea," said Mom.

My father hollered again. "Where's my bloody bin of teans?"

My mother covered her mouth and turned away, but it was too late—I'd caught the smirk, and once I caught something, I wouldn't let it go.

"Bin of teans!" I sang. "Bin of teans! Where's my bloody bin of teans?"

My mother shushed me as she emptied a can of Heinz baked beans into a saucepan.

"Bin of teans! Bin of teans! Where's my bloody bin of teans?" I sang again.

"Shhh, Kit, seriously. Be quiet," said my mother, but I could tell she thought it was funny.

I turned a pot upside down and sang the song again, pounding out an accompanying rhythm with a wooden spoon.

"Kit." My mother giggled. "Stop it."

I liked it when she laughed. So I stood on top of the pot and threw my arms in the air and sang in my best Julie Andrews voice, "Bin of teans! Bin of teans! Where's my bloody bin of teans?"

And there he was. In the doorway. "What's that bloody racket? Can't a man watch the TV in peace?"

My mother went all slumpy and saggy. Like a deflated balloon. "It's almost done, Phonse." She sighed. "Sit down at the table and I'll dish it up."

"I've been waiting for hours," he said, stumbling through the mess of pots and pans. "Hours and hours. I'm hungry."

"It hasn't been hours," Mom said. "It's been about ten minutes."

My father sat down hard in his chair.

"I got you the ones you like," Mom said. "The ones with bits of bacon mixed in."

"Well, whoopdi-bloody-doo," he said.

"That's rude," I said in a matter-of-fact way.

"Yeah, it is," agreed Mom.

"Stop harrashin' me," Dad said.

"Stop harrashin' me," I said, mimicking my father's gruff smoker's voice.

Mom flashed me a warning look.

Dad stared at me and then at my mom. "Fishing twenny-four/seven to pervide for you two," he grumbled, "and whadoo I get?"

My mother put the bowl in front of him. "Lunch. Here it is. Now eat it."

"I want more than lunch," he said. "What I want is re*speck*!' He tried to hit the table with his fist but missed and ended up punching himself in the crotch.

My mother shook her head impatiently. "Eat your beans, Alphonsus."

"Don't tell me what to do, woman."

Mom ran some water in the empty pot and stared out the kitchen window. "I'm so tired of this."

"I'm tired too," said my father. "Tired of workin' my fingers to the bone. Twenny-four/seven, I work. Twenny-four/seven."

My mother reeled around, her eyes so wild I thought for sure her voice would be loud. I even covered my ears. But what came out was a low growl. "The only thing you do twenty-four/seven is—"

And then she looked at me. And stopped talking.

My parents stared at each other like they were having some kind of cowboy showdown. There were beans stuck to my father's chin. It was gross. So I put the biggest pot over my head.

I wondered when the staring contest would end. Then I heard the kitchen chair being pushed back. I peeked out. Dad was attempting to stand. He rocked a bit to the left, then he rocked a bit to the right. He looked down at me. He seemed confused, like he knew me but wasn't sure from where. Then he picked up the bowl of beans and threw it against the wall.

We stared, stunned, at the mess.

"You raving lunatic!" my mother yelled.

A sticky, gloopy brown mess slid down the wall. It looked like poop. It made me feel sick. So I ran out the door and down the dirt road. I only had to pass three houses to get to Nan's. The first was Ms. Bartlett's. The next house after that belonged to my best friend, Anne-Marie Munro. She was outside playing in the dirt as I raced by.

"I'm going to Nan's," I yelled. "By myself!"

Anne-Marie looked stunned, then called, "Watch out for Fisty Hinks!"

When I passed the next house with its weathered gray clapboard and twitching curtains, I ran extra fast. Fisty Hinks didn't like kids. If he heard them, he'd come out with his hand balled up in a fist. "I'll getcha, ya little buggers," he'd shout.

Nan's was the last house of all. She didn't ask me where my parents were or why I was by myself. The only thing she asked was did I want one slice of homemade bread with molasses or two. She made me a cup of weak tea with loads of milk and lots of sugar. She called it "baby tea." It fixed my tummy.

I went to Nan's lots after that. She was always at the stove, sweating over partridgeberry jam, or at the table, making bread. Sometimes she'd knead the dough so hard my cup of tea would quiver and shake. Nan's apron was brown with blue flowers. It tied around her waist, cutting right into her middle so that a small roll of fat bulged out over the top. Nan wasn't a big woman. But she was sturdy...solid...strong. The strongest woman I had ever known.

Nan was always singing. My favorite was the one about a man and his horse. The horse was named Kit, like me. One day, the man used the frozen pond as a shortcut and the ice broke.

I raised an alarm you could hear for a mile
And neighbors turned up in a very short while
You can always rely on the Oldfords and Whites
To render assistance in all your bad plights

To help a poor neighbor is part of their lives
And the same I can say for their children and wives.

Every time I heard this song, I shivered. That poor mare must have been chilled to the bone. So I imagined drying her with my hair dryer and brushing her mane until she looked like one of my sparkly plastic ponies. But when I hear the song now, I don't think about ponies. I think about neighbors…and how important they are.

I SHOWED UP at Nan's pissed off and out of breath after the fight with Dad. She barely glanced up from her knitting. It wasn't that she didn't care—far from it. My bursting through her door in a huff was a regular occurrence, that's all. She was used to it.

"What was it this time?" she asked.

I leaned over and kissed her on the cheek. "We got into a fight."

What I loved about Nan was that I didn't have to pretend. Even though he was her only son, I could rant about my dad till I was blue in the face. It made a nice change from playing happy families with my mother at home.

"A fight?" she said, her knitting needles moving at lightning speed. "A fight about what?"

"*The Old Man and the Sea.*"

The clickity-clack of the needles stopped and Nan looked up at me. "The who and the what?"

The look on her face was classic—the squinty eyes, the scrunched-up nose, the wrinkled forehead. She was my instant mood improver. Bad day? Just add Nan. I leaned over and kissed her again. "Never mind," I said. "It's not important. Cup of tea?"

She nodded.

I filled up the kettle. "Whatcha knitting?"

The clickity-clack resumed. "Mittens."

"Mittens? In June?"

"There's a church fundraiser in September. I'm going to try to make thirty pairs."

"Thirty? That'll take all summer."

Nan shrugged. "What else am I going to do? It's not like I'll be jetting off to Paris or anything."

"Who'd want to go to Paris anyway?" I snorted.

Nan looked up, this time surprised. "I would, for one!"

I couldn't picture Nan posing for a photo in front of the Eiffel Tower but didn't say so. "Not me," I said. "I'd take Parsons Bay any day. Especially in summer."

Nan tutted and shook her head. "You're sixteen years old, Kit. Where's your sense of adventure?"

"Trust me," I said. "My home life's enough of an adventure."

Nan sighed. "I suppose so."

"And anyway," I continued, "why would I go to some foreign country where I can't understand a thing anybody's saying when I can stay here in this kitchen all summer and help you make mittens?"

"Ha!" said Nan. "You? Knit?"

"Why not?" I said. "You can teach me."

Nan put down her knitting. "You, my duckie, don't have the patience for knitting."

"Yes I do! I have lots of patience."

"If you say so."

I went back to the stove. "Geez, your kettle takes ages to boil."

Nan laughed. "See?"

I smiled. "You can read me like a book, Nan."

"I know you better than you know yourself," she said, moving from her rocker to a kitchen chair.

I poured the tea. "Okay then, smarty-pants," I teased. "If you know me so well, what am I thinking?"

Nan closed her eyes. "Let me see…it's coming to me now…I can feel it…yes!" She opened her eyes. "They're in the tin."

I reached for Nan's ancient biscuit tin and opened the lid. "The fact that I like tea buns hardly requires psychic ability," I said. "I eat them every time I'm here."

"Still," said Nan, "there's no denying I know you well."

"Like the back of your hand," I said with a mouthful of bun.

We sat quietly for a while as Nan slurped her tea and seagulls cried outside the kitchen window.

"So what *will* you do this summer?" asked Nan when her cup was drained.

I washed down my last mouthful of bun with the sugary tea. "Enjoy the peace and quiet."

Nan squinted at me again. "Peace and quiet?"

"Yeah. It's almost fishing season, remember?"

"What does that have to do with peace and quiet?" asked Nan. "If anything, fishing season is the noisiest time of the year."

"You mean the most *wonderful* time of the year."

Nan laughed. "And why is that?"

"Because Dad'll be gone! Out on the boat! All day, every day!" I burst into song. "*It's the most wonderful time of the year.*"

Nan wasn't laughing anymore. "Oh, love."

"What's wrong?

"I just wish things were different for you, that's all."

I shrugged. "Don't worry about me, Nan. He's a pain in the arse, but it's nothing I can't handle."

Nan shook her head. "If only I—"

I stuck my fingers in my ears. "Lalala. Can't hear you, Nan."

"I'm serious, Kit. I must have gone wrong somewhere."

"I'm not having this conversation, Nan. You are an amazing grandmother and I bet you were an amazing mother too. The way he acts has nothing to do with you. Got it?"

Nan reached for her knitting. "Grab a pair of needles out of my basket and choose a ball of wool."

My face lit up. "Really?"

"You'll need something to do during all that peace and quiet."

I picked yellow, to match the walls.

BUT THINGS WEREN'T going to be nice and quiet after all. The summer of 1992 had barely begun when the Newfoundland government shut down the cod fishery. They called it a moratorium. No fishing for two years. It was all anyone could talk about. Or, in my parents' case, fight about. "Phonse, for the love of God, stop sitting on your arse and complaining about it. It'll do us no good."

Dad ignored the plateful of food in front of him and concentrated on what was in his glass. "Goddammit, Emily, what am I supposed to do?"

Mom said Dad should look into aid packages, weekly payments for unemployed fishermen. But he wouldn't hear of it.

"I'm not going on the package. You won't see me living off handouts from the bloody government. No way."

"There's nothing wrong with accepting a bit of help, Phonse. The government is setting up programs, helping fisherman retrain…"

"I'm forty-bloody-three years old, Em. What am I going to retrain as…a goddamn doctor? A friggin' lawyer? I'm a cod fisherman, like my dad and his dad before him. We make our living off the sea." Dad violently stubbed out his cigarette on his plate. "It's the damn seals. Eating every bit of fish out there."

My mother snatched my father's dirty plate and threw an ashtray down in front of him. "I heard someone on the CBC say that the seals may not be the problem after all."

"And what genius said that?" said Dad, lighting up another cigarette.

"Someone from the Department of Fisheries, I think."

"Well, whoopdi-bloody-doo! It was probably the same arsehole who said seals don't eat cod. Well, I agree with Captain Morrissey Johnson. You know what he said? He said, 'Well, I know they don't eat turnips.'"

Mom collected the dirty dishes. "I'm just tellin' ya what I heard."

Dad poured another glass of the golden stuff from his bottle. He didn't mix it with Pepsi this time. "And the friggin' foreign overfishing...that's depleting our cod stocks too. We're being fished dry."

Mom slammed the stack of dirty plates back down on the table. "Well, what are we going to do, Phonse? Tell me. What are we going to do?"

As their voices got louder and louder, I felt smaller and smaller. The more they yelled, the less they saw me, and the less they saw me, the madder I got.

"Would anyone like to hear *my* thoughts?" I asked.

They looked surprised to see me, as if I had just showed up.

"Well?"

Dad gave a little snort of amusement.

I gritted my teeth. "What's so funny?"

"Nothing, sweetheart," said Mom. "Sit down. We'd love to hear your thoughts."

I looked at my dad. He folded his arms and smirked. "Okay then," he said. "Enlighten us. How are we going to get out of this mess?"

"Phonse, please," said Mom.

"Come on, Little Miss Know-It-All," he said, ignoring my mother. "You usually have an answer for everything. Let's hear it."

"I was just going to say that maybe you could go farther out from port, try scallop fishing. That's what Tracy Barter's dad is going to do."

Dad burst out laughing. "Scallop fishing! Hmm, let me think about that. Scallop fishing means new equipment, and new equipment means money, and money, well, we're kind of low on that. Brilliant idea, Einstein."

"It was just an idea," I muttered.

My father finished his drink and poured another. "Be a good girl, Kitty, and run along to your room. Your mother and me have important things to talk about. Grown-up things."

I gripped the side of the table. "Don't be so patronizing."

"Ooh, big word," he said with a chuckle.

"You are *so* immature," I yelled.

Dad stopped laughing. "Don't you raise your voice at me, young lady."

My mother stared at the tablecloth and sighed. "Just go, Kit."

I gave the table a shove as I pushed my chair back. Dad's whiskey bottle wobbled back and forth, so I shoved the table again, quick and hard. He caught the bottle just in time.

"Go, Kit." My mother's voice was urgent this time.

I did as I was told.

I could still hear them, even with my bedroom door closed. *Mumble, mumble, arse mumble, mumble, goddammit, mumble, mumble, fish...*I grabbed my coat and went to Nan's. But for the first time, I felt no sense of escape. As she buttered my bread she sang:

What ever happened to the gold in the water?
That swam into our nets and kept our spirits strong
*   and free?*
What will become of our sons and our daughters
who trusted us to know that there would always be
gold in the water...the reason for living,
the reason for giving up our lives unto the sea
Whatever happened to the gold in the water?
What will become of you and me?

And for the first time, I yelled at my grandmother. "All anybody can talk about is stupid fish!"

I stormed out and went to Anne-Marie's. "C'mon," I said. "Let's go up to the top of the cliff."

But before we trekked up the path, I slipped back into my house. Mom and Dad were still at it. *Mumble, mumble, fish, mumble, mumble, crap...*I crept up the stairs, stepping over the squeaky third step, and snuck into my parents' room. I slid two cigarettes out of a package on Dad's dresser and tiptoed back downstairs. As I opened the front door, I heard Mom clearly. "Then we'll have to leave Parsons Bay. There's nothing here. I'll talk to Iggy. We can stay with him in St. John's. We've better chances of finding work there."

My heart sank. Iggy? I didn't want to live with Iggy. I'd barely said two words to him since I was twelve. I mean, I'd seen him a year ago at his wife's funeral, but that didn't really count. And what about Nan? I didn't want to leave Nan.

Instead of going out the front door, I took three steps backward, nipped into the living room and took two cans of beer from Dad's stash in the liquor cabinet.

Up on the cliff, Anne-Marie and I sat on the grass, staring at the stolen goods.

Anne-Marie looked at me as if I were nuts. "What are we supposed to do with this?"

"Um, let me think," I said. "My guess is the beer is for drinking and the cigarettes are for smoking."

"Ha ha," said Anne-Marie. "You're hilarious." She pulled her long brown hair into a ponytail and fastened it with an elastic she had around her wrist. "I'm not touching that stuff. I have to get up early to build a shed."

"A shed?"

"Yes, a shed. Last week, I designed it. This week, I build it. With Dad's help, of course."

"Tomboy," I said.

"Yep," said Anne-Marie with pride. "And the day after, we're installing a bidet at Ms. Bartlett's."

"A what?"

"A bidet. You install it next to your toilet. You sit on it after you do your business and water sprays up to clean your, you know, area."

"So it's a fancy arse cleaner."

Anne-Marie laughed. "Yeah, basically. Ms. Bartlett ordered it from the mainland. She says they're very useful."

"I hope she's prepared for the lineups outside her door. The entire population of Parsons Bay will want to have a go. Except me. I'll stick to toilet paper, thank you very much."

"Anyway," said Anne-Marie, "the whole installation sounds complicated, so no booze or smokes for me. I need to stay in top physical form."

"It's *one* beer and *one* cigarette," I said. "It's not going to make that much of a difference."

Anne-Marie folded her arms. "Like I said, you do what you like. But I'm not touching that stuff. Why did you even steal it?"

I wasn't really sure. I felt like I was punishing my parents in a way, but then again, it was kind of pointless because they'd probably never find out. Still, I felt some satisfaction in depleting Dad's stash of smokes and booze, even just a little bit.

"Well?" asked Anne-Marie. "What's up?"

"We're probably moving," I said.

"What? Moving? When? Where?"

"St. John's. To live with Uncle Iggy."

Anne-Marie was shocked. "I don't believe it."

"Believe it," I said, my voice shaking. "Because it's probably going to happen."

"But why?"

"Because of the stupid moratorium. You're lucky your dad's a carpenter."

"Oh, Kit."

"It's a disaster. We'll probably be gone by the end of the month."

Anne-Marie put her arm around me. "It'll be okay. St. John's is only five hours away, and your Uncle Iggy's cool. Remember how he'd take us for ice cream whenever he came to visit?"

"Yeah, but I've barely seen him since he went off to university and got married and stuff."

"You'll get to know him again, Kit. And isn't he the one with the big fancy house? You'll be living the high life."

"His wife just died last year, remember? Living with a drunk is bad enough. I don't want to live with someone in mourning as well."

My head was spinning. New place. New school. New friends. I hoped Dad would disagree with Mom. I hoped he'd put his foot down and say we wouldn't move. After all, Nan was his mother. How could he leave her?

"Let's go home," said Anne-Marie. "You don't really want this stuff. Leave it here for some losers who really need it."

We were about to get up when Will Hanrahan and Toby Burt came off the trailhead.

"Speaking of losers," I said. Anne-Marie laughed.

"Well, well, well," said Will. "It's little Kit Ryan and Anne-Marie Munro. When did the two of you pick up smoking and drinking?"

"Ages ago," I lied.

"Aren't you a bit young?" asked Will with a smirk.

"We're only a year younger than you," said Anne-Marie.

"That one year makes a huge difference," said Toby, "as far as maturity goes."

"So why don't you two leave the smokes and the beer for the big boys," said Will, "and run along home?"

I reached out and grabbed a beer. Anne-Marie's mouth dropped open. I popped the tab and forced my face to stay normal as I took a sip. I tossed the other can to Will. "Here, you guys can split this if you want. Anne-Marie and I have already had a couple."

Anne-Marie's eyes were huge.

"Do you want some of this?" I asked her. "Or have you had enough tonight?"

"Enough," she spluttered. "I've had enough."

Will lit up a cigarette and asked if I needed a light.

"Sure." I picked up a cigarette and tried to hold it as naturally as possible, mimicking my dad, who was never without one. I looked at the cigarette between my fingers and thought of Dad's disgusting fingers, yellowed with nicotine stains, and I knew before I even took a puff of my first cigarette ever that it would be my last.

UNFORTUNATELY, DAD DIDN'T disagree with Mom. Within three weeks of the announcement, we were packing up and moving to St. John's. It was a sad day when Dad sold his boat. Fishing boats weren't in high demand since the moratorium, and he had to practically give it away, selling it for way less than it was worth. I was surprised at how hard it hit me. I mean, I knew *he* was attached to it—I just didn't realize I was as well.

I was ten years old before Dad took me out on his boat. All the other kids in Parsons Bay had been on their dads' boats since they were little. Some of them were even working on them part-time. It wasn't Dad's fault. Mom would never let me go. Dad would laugh it off to his friends. "It's the wife…just a tad overprotective." But at home he would say, "Goddammit, Em, she's my daughter. I am not going to let any harm come to her."

But Mom would say, "As long as Johnnie Walker and Captain Morgan are part of your crew, you will not be taking my daughter out on that boat. You can't be trusted. You're irresponsible. I don't want to see my Kit washing up on the shore."

My father named his boat after something my grandpa Skipper said when I was little. Skipper was my mom's dad, and he drove us all nuts by constantly complaining about his many ailments. One day he was moaning about a black spot on his big toe. Mom said it was a wart. Skipper said it was cancer.

I asked Mom if he was going to die. She said, "Kit, your grandfather is a hypochondriac."

I asked Dad if Grandpa Skipper needed a doctor. He said, "Kit, what your grandfather needs is a good kick up the arse."

I went to my bedroom and got my magic kit. "Skipper? Want me to magic it away?"

"No harm in trying," he sighed.

I came up with a magical cure-all chant and knelt down beside the ottoman where his foot was resting. With his big toe at close range, I hesitated. It was huge, and the nail was long and yellowed. Instinctively I held my breath. I knew all too well the smell that came from the big rubber hip waders he wore every day. The whole porch reeked of them, so I could only imagine what the foot itself smelled like. But I had a job to do. I raised my magic wand. "Abracadabra Alakazot, please get rid of that big ugly spot!"

Mom rolled her eyes. Dad laughed his head off. Skipper thanked me and went to sleep.

The next day Skipper gathered the whole family around. "Our Kit has magical healing powers!" he declared. "Look! It's gone! I never saw the likes of that in my whole entire life. She's a charmer, I tell ya, a charmer."

"What a load of horseshit," said Dad. "Sure I can still see it there, plain as day."

"Well, I didn't say it was *completely* gone," huffed Skipper. "But it has shrunk. Sure it's practically invisible! Can't you see that? Are you blind or what?"

Dad snorted. "I'm not the one that's blind."

My mother shot him a look. "Okay, Phonse, that's enough." She took a close look at Skipper's toe. "Well, will you look at that. It *has* shrunk a bit."

"My little charmer," said Skipper, looking at me with a big smile.

After that, he had me curing all of his friends. I abracadabraed Mrs. Ryan's stomachache and alakazammed old Dick Mulligan's boil. I even hocus-pocused Mrs. Pope's colitis. And afterward, every one of them claimed there was an improvement. Anne-Marie teased me, saying Fisty Hinks wanted his arthritis charmed away because his fist wasn't as tight as it used to be. Dad thought the whole thing was hysterical. That year, when he branched out on his own and bought his very own fishing boat, he named it *Kitty Charmer*.

When I was little and my friends asked why I had never been out on the boat, I pretended it was my choice. "Why would I want to go out on an old boat and come back stinking of fish?" Then one Saturday morning it happened. "C'mon," said Dad. "It's time you came aboard the *Kitty Charmer*." I looked at Mom. She looked away.

Dad and I walked to the cove. I wondered if girls my age still held their father's hands. Not that I would or anything. I just wondered.

As soon as I stood on the wharf, my legs went to jelly. It was a floating dock and a bit bouncy. I looked down at the water. Millions of minnows swam happily by. I wondered if there were sharks in Newfoundland.

"C'mon, Kitty."

Dad had already climbed on deck. He grabbed my arm and pulled me up and over the side of the boat. I could smell alcohol on his breath. I wondered which one of his crew members it was, Johnnie Walker or Captain Morgan. They may have been just names on bottles, but those bottles held my Dad's liquid gold. And that made them dangerous.

While Dad prepared the boat, I peered over the side and looked at the dingy off-white paint. It was chipped and rusty. But the words *Kitty Charmer* were in perfect shape. They were the same sky blue that spattered Dad's coveralls. He always protected those words. Always seemed to be touching them up. The *Kitty Charmer* really meant something to him.

I reached over the edge and touched the *K*. It was shiny and smooth. The boat started with a jolt. I grabbed the side. The smell of diesel and fish made me feel sick. I clung to the side. Dad picked up speed, and soon the fresh salty air made me feel better. *I could get used to this*, I thought. *It's like an amusement-park ride.* But still, my knuckles were white.

Out in the middle of nowhere, Dad cut the engine. "Kitty, are you going to move from that spot or what? You're like a statue." I looked over the side and into the Atlantic. "Kitty," Dad said again, "come and see how these nets work."

Can't be trusted...irresponsible...Kit washing up on the shore.

I was frozen. Dad came up behind me. "Kitty, love. I'm not going to let anything happen to you."

The boat rocked back and forth. "I'm scared," I said.

"Your old man's here, Kitty." He put his hands gently over mine. They were rough and cold, but they made me feel warm. How was that possible? "Now come over and see how these nets work." He took me by the hand and didn't let go for the longest time. Even when he was showing me the nets, he did it with his free hand. And when he eventually needed to use both hands, he put mine safely back on the side of the boat first. But soon I felt able to let go. I even explored a bit. "You got your sea legs pretty quick, Kitty. You're a fisherman's daughter, that's for sure."

Dad took me down below. I knew there was a down below because Anne-Marie had told me about the one on her Uncle Bill's boat. She said there were bunk beds. She said she'd slept on the top bunk. I asked her why on earth she would want to sleep on a stupid boat. I told her that sleeping on a rocking boat would make me sick to my stomach, but she said it was awesome, that the waves rocked her to sleep. So down below on my own father's boat, I immediately looked for the bunks. And there they were, top and bottom.

"Go ahead," Dad said. "Give it a try."

"Okay," I sighed, as if it was a chore, as if I was doing him a favor. I sat on the bottom bunk for a moment. When Dad wasn't looking, I lay down. I stared at the bunk above me. Then, when Dad busied himself making tea, I climbed into the top bunk. I had never been on the top bunk of a bunk bed, let alone one on a boat. I closed my eyes and felt the waves rocking me back and forth. I stayed there until Dad called me to the table for lunch.

He took two sandwiches out of a little fridge, one for me and one for him. They were tuna, which I didn't like, but I didn't say anything. He told me stories from his fishing trips. Stories about the size of some of the fish he had caught, stories about the other men who fished with him and stories about storms, dangerous storms, where men had gone overboard.

"You can swim, right?" I asked.

"Nah," he said. "Never learned. And it's just as well… if you end up in those cold waters, you're a goner. The sooner the better, if you ask me." I shivered just thinking about it. Then he pulled a Kit Kat from his pocket and we shared it. "Look, Kitty," he said, pointing out the porthole. "A minke whale."

I'd seen lots of whales before. From the top of the cliff. But this was close. This was magic.

Dad looked at his watch. "Better get back. Your mother will wonder what's happened to us."

My mother. I had missed out on so much because of her.

Dad let me take the wheel on the way back. He called me Captain. Captain Kitty.

Mom was waiting on the wharf. I could tell by the look on her face that she was not happy. So I skipped off the boat with a big smile, holding Dad's hand, telling her what a grand time we'd had, how I'd never had so much fun.

"You were gone so long," she said. "I was worried sick." She reached for me, but I turned away and held Dad's hand tighter.

"C'mon, Dad. Let's go home."

Things were good between my dad and me for exactly six days. But then he and Mom got into a humongous fight about the price of Pepsi. Mom said he bought too much of it, that it was too expensive and he shouldn't buy it anymore. He said he needed it and for her to mind her own goddamn business. But she kept going on and on about it, and Dad exploded. He screamed until his voice went hoarse, and one of the things he screamed was *bitch*. It made me feel sick, but what made me feel even sicker was the sound of Mom sobbing in the bathroom.

Still, the memory of that day on the *Kitty Charmer* stood out as a good one. And now it was being sold. Now it was going to disappear. Along with the rest of my life in Parsons Bay.

ONCE I'D FINISHED packing, I called Anne-Marie. It was time to say goodbye. I asked her to meet me at our usual spot. I was going to miss that grassy place at the top of the cliff. We'd been meeting there for years, and long before we should have been. Two young girls playing on dangerous bluffs high above the rocky coastline could have spelled disaster. But we didn't care. I would tell Mom I was going down to Nan's, but instead I'd go to Anne-Marie's and throw pebbles at her bedroom window. She'd crawl out and up the cliff we'd go, knowing full well we'd be in big trouble if we were ever caught. Getting to the trail was tricky. Dad's boat was tied up close to the trailhead. If he wasn't out fishing, we'd have to wait until he was down in the hull of the boat, and then we'd run past, get on the trail and beat it up the hill until we were out of sight. We'd spend hours up there, Anne-Marie and me. We'd gossip about everyone in town. We'd talk about Fisty Hinks and why he yelled at kids who passed by. Will Hanrahan said that Fisty once had a wife and daughter, but he killed them, chopped them up in a million pieces and buried them in front of his house, and now he didn't want people walking on their graves. Anne-Marie and I decided there was no way that could be true. We figured if Fisty was mean enough to chop up his wife and kid in a million pieces, he probably wouldn't care who walked on their graves. The little kids in town believed that Fisty ate little children and that's why you had to run—if he caught you, into the oven you'd go. Mom told us to leave the poor man alone, that he was just a sad and lonely man whose sadness and loneliness made him grumpy. We didn't like that theory—it was too boring to believe.

We would talk about my dad too. Anne-Marie knew he was a drunk. She promised she'd never tell anyone. I could really trust Anne-Marie. And now I had to say goodbye.

I looked down at the winding trail, and when I saw Anne-Marie running toward me, carrying a worn tartan blanket under her arm, I wished things didn't have to change.

We flattened a patch of overgrown grass and spread out the blanket.

"Is the shed done?" I asked.

"Yep. We're painting it now." She pointed to red spatters on her overalls. "Like the color?"

"Yeah. Looks good."

We flopped down onto the blanket. The earth was damp and the air was filled with mist.

"Stinks of fish around here today," said Anne-Marie.

I licked salt off my lips and breathed in deeply, inhaling the ocean air. I held it as long as I could, but sixty seconds later I had to exhale. Nothing lasts forever.

"So you're gonna come back to visit, right?" said Anne-Marie.

I traced the yellow threads of the blanket with my finger. "If we can afford it," I said.

"A bus ticket doesn't cost that much, does it?"

"The way my parents talk, you'd think it was a small fortune. They've already told me not to set my sights on too many visits back to Parsons Bay."

"Do you really have to go?" asked Anne-Marie. "Can't you stay with your nan?"

"I already asked. I practically begged them. They said no. They said Nan's too old to look after a teenager. They said she's slowing down. And I said that if she's slowing down, we should stay in Parsons Bay and look after her. But they won't listen. They've made up their minds."

We could hear the waves crashing a hundred feet below us.

"It's going to suck," I said. "I don't want to go to a new school."

"At least you're starting at the beginning of the year and not in the middle of it."

"Yeah, but now I have to spend the rest of the summer in St. John's. With no friends and nothing to do."

"I'm sure you'll meet new people, Kit."

"I don't want to meet new people. Especially townies. They're probably all snobs. They'll just think I'm some stupid baygirl."

"Maybe they'll think you're quaint," said Anne-Marie.

I frowned at her. "Quaint?" I ran my fingers through my hair. "Maybe I should get a haircut before I go. Something stylish."

"Your hair is fine, Kit."

"No, it's not. It's boring and straight and dull. Maybe I should get blond highlights. I read that golden tones bring out blue eyes."

"I like the color of your hair."

"Dad says it looks like dirty dishwater."

"And you believe him?"

I wound a strand around my finger. "No, but—"

"Your father is full of crap, Kit. Don't let him get to you. And anyway, do you really think making new friends is going to depend on your hairstyle?"

"I just want to fit in."

"You will."

"I hope so."

"I'm kind of jealous, actually."

"Really? Why?"

"Because St. John's has two big shopping malls," she said. "And movie theaters and museums. It'll be exciting. There's never anything to do here. Parsons Bay sucks."

I stood up and walked toward the cliff's edge. A whale-watching boat was leaving the dock. Tourists with binoculars filled the deck. Some had traveled from faraway places to experience Parsons Bay—the rugged coastline, the wildlife, the peace and quiet.

Anne-Marie came up behind me. I was glad it was misty. My face was soaked.

"We'd better go now," I said.

We hugged each other tightly, then headed back toward home. There was one more person I needed to say goodbye to.

MOST PEOPLE USED the doorbell at Ms. Bartlett's house, but I preferred the knocker. It was a goblin. Ms. Bartlett called him "the bronzed brute."

"I'm going to miss that goblin," I said when Ms. Bartlett opened the door.

"Oh, Kit." She gave me a big hug and led me through to her living room.

I was going to say, "I like your dress," but I wasn't sure if it actually was a dress because it was all silky and flowing, like a robe. Dad probably would have burst out laughing and called her the hippie-dippie freak show. He thought she was weird, but I loved her.

"I like what you're wearing," I said.

Ms. Bartlett gathered up the billows of brilliant blue material and sat down on the couch. "Thank you, Kit. It's a kaftan. I found it in Morocco."

Ms. Bartlett's house was full of artifacts and knick-knacks from around the globe—African masks, Japanese wall hangings, Persian rugs. Mom told me once that Ms. Bartlett could travel the world whenever she felt like it because she had lots of money. Ms. Bartlett's father left Parsons Bay to start a business in the city. Soon he owned all the Bartlett's department stores in Atlantic Canada. When he died he left the business to his children, but Ms. Bartlett wanted no part of it. Mom told me Ms. Bartlett had laughed and said, "Can you picture me in a business suit?" Her siblings bought her out and she moved back to the Bartlett family home in Parsons Bay. The town gossip was that Ms. Bartlett was sitting on a small fortune. Mom didn't doubt it. She said that if you could afford to waste your money on a six-foot-tall sculpture of a giraffe, then you must have plenty of it.

"I wish I could travel," I said as I made myself comfy on the couch.

"Maybe you will someday."

I reached into the candy dish on the coffee table. I didn't have to ask.

"Mmm, Turkish delight."

"I'll send you some when you're in St. John's."

I secretly hoped that if Ms. Bartlett knew how badly I wanted to stay in Parsons Bay, she'd offer to let me stay with her. So I built up my case. "I don't want to go to St. John's, Ms. Bartlett. For one thing, I don't want to leave Nan. I'll miss her so much. And I really, really, really don't want to go to a new school. Especially a big-city school. It's going to be terrible."

"I'd love to have you stay with me, Kit, but I can't."

I didn't know what to say, so I just took another Turkish delight and looked at the rug.

"There are some things that can't be changed, Kit."

"Then I guess this is goodbye," I mumbled.

Ms. Bartlett stood up. "Come here, Kit." She took my hand and pulled me to my feet. "I learned a wonderful word when I was with the Apache Indians down in Arizona. *Egogahan*. It means 'until we meet again.'"

"Then egogahan, Ms. Bartlett."

Ms. Bartlett held me tight. "Egogahan, Kit."

TWO
Poor Old Dead Aunt Margie

We drove across the province in our old Buick, a flatbed trailer hitched to the back with Dad's smelly old recliner strapped to the roof of the car. We'd sold practically everything we owned, but Dad wouldn't part with that stupid chair, and I dreaded pulling in to Uncle Iggy's fancy neighborhood with it attached to our car.

Dad chain-smoked the whole way. I spent part of the journey with my head out the window, like a dog, just to get a breath of fresh air. The Trans-Canada Highway was boring, the only excitement being an unplanned stop to yield for a herd of caribou. I slept for ages, and when I woke up we were in an industrial area just outside the city limits.

"How long until we're at Uncle Iggy's?" I asked.

"About fifteen minutes," Mom said.

Dad looked at me in the rearview mirror. "Make that thirty," he said. A few minutes later we were driving through downtown. Colorful row houses lined the streets, their bright paint reminding me of the homes along the coastline of Parsons Bay. Dad parked at the harbor. "Just going for a quick one at the Ship." Mom didn't comment. She never did. But it was a wonder she didn't fog up the whole car with the amount of air she expelled from her lungs.

Some boys in baggy jeans were skateboarding up and down the harborfront. One of them had a mohawk. "What a state," Mom said. "They look like a bunch of thugs." But I thought they looked cool.

I rolled down the window. The harbor's fishy air was like a little bit of home. In the distance, a cruise ship appeared. It was massive. I wondered how it would fit through the narrows without hitting the cliffs on either side. I settled in to watch the whole thing. But Dad came back too soon.

"What a bunch of dirtbags," he said, pointing to the skateboarders. "Look at the size of their pants. Have they never heard of a belt?"

"I think they look cool," I said.

"If you ever bring the likes of that home, Kitty, I'll probably keel over and die."

"Now there's an idea," I muttered.

"Let's get going, Phonse," said Mom. "Iggy's waiting."

Suddenly I didn't want to leave. Going to Iggy's meant starting over. And I didn't want to. Not yet. I needed more time.

Dad put the key in the ignition. The second the car started, I took a big breath, holding in the ocean air as if I'd never have the opportunity again, as if moving to Uncle Iggy's was the end of my life as I knew it. We drove up Hill O'Chips, one of the steepest streets in St. John's. I didn't exhale till we reached the top.

The colors of downtown faded quickly. Before I knew it, we were in a dingy neighborhood.

"What are we doing here?" I asked. "This doesn't look like Uncle Iggy's neighborhood."

"It is now," said Dad. "So much for Mr. Engineering Degree and his successful life."

Mom shot Dad a dirty look. "Now, Phonse, we all know how hard it is when a man loses his job, don't we?"

"He lost his job?" I asked. "How come no one told me? Why did he move?"

"Because he can't afford that fancy house anymore. Lost that high-paying job of his because of depression or something," said Dad. "Probably just as well. A big house like that for one person is a waste of space."

"So how come no one told me?" I repeated.

"There's been a lot going on, Kit," said Mom. "Do you have to know every detail?"

"Yes," I snapped. "I do. Especially when one of the 'details' involves me moving to this sucky neighborhood."

"It's a fine neighborhood," said Mom.

"Not!" my father snorted.

"This isn't funny, Phonse."

Dad was driving slowly, and Mom was looking at house numbers.

"This is it," said Mom.

We pulled up to a small, scruffy-looking house.

"You didn't tell me because you knew I wouldn't have come if I'd known Uncle Iggy wasn't living in his big house anymore."

My mother got out of the car and opened my door. "We didn't tell you because it didn't matter. We were moving no matter what. Now get out of the car, put a smile on your face, and come say hello to your uncle Iggy."

I had to hide my shock when I saw him. Cool, hip Uncle Iggy was gone and in his place was a sloppy, disheveled bum. Instead of his usual crisp blue jeans and fitted T-shirts, Uncle Iggy was wearing a stained sweater and baggy sweatpants. Stuff you'd wear to bed. Stuff you'd wear if you had a messy painting job to do. Stuff that's not good enough for anything else. And his hair used to be messy on purpose. Now it was just plain messy...and a bit greasy too. He looked hopeless. I guess that's what happens when a tractor-trailer crashes into your wife's car, leaving you a widower in your early thirties.

"Hi, Kit. Wow, you've really changed." He gave me an awkward hug. Years ago he would have grabbed my hands and whirled me around, saying, "You're my favorite niece, you know," and I would have answered, "I'm your *only* niece!" It used to be our own little joke. Uncle Iggy didn't look like he joked much anymore.

Uncle Iggy's house was as shabby as he was. All his great furniture from the big house was nowhere to be seen. The only thing I recognized was the old leather chair he'd bought in his university days. Aunt Margie had teased him, saying that once they were married she wouldn't allow the chair in the new house. But she did, even though it was well worn and had a few burn holes in the arm. Now there were so many burn holes that it wasn't a leather chair dotted with a few burn holes but a big burn hole dotted with bits of leather chair. Uncle Iggy had always been a smoker, but this was ridiculous. Even the walls and ceilings were sooty. If I was going to be living in a giant ashtray for God knows how long, I figured I might as well start smoking myself.

Uncle Iggy led us into the kitchen for tea. Paint was peeling off the walls, the cabinets were missing their handles, the faucet had a steady drip, and the linoleum was peppered with his signature burn holes.

"Like what you've done to the place," said Dad. Mom slapped him on the arm.

At least your ugly, stinky chair will fit in with the decor, I thought.

"I'm only having a lark, missus," said Dad. "Iggy here knows that, don't you, Iggy?"

Iggy looked down. "Oh, yeah, sure." My heart sank. He looked so meek.

"Where's all your nice furniture, Ig?" Mom asked.

He shook his head. "I...I couldn't stand to look at it."

Mom reached for his hand.

We sat at the kitchen table under a cloud of awkward silence. Uncle Iggy looked at me. "Sorry to be such a downer, Kit."

"It's okay," I said.

"I got your room all ready for you," he said, a note of hope in his voice.

"Oh, thanks."

"You'll be sleeping in Margie's sewing room," he said. Then he added, as if I'd be pleased, "And it still smells of her."

I almost choked on my tea.

"Well, whoopdi-bloody-doo!" boomed Dad, with a smirk. "You'll be sleeping in your poor old dead aunt Margie's sewing room. And it still smells of her!"

Mom shot him a look and then plastered a smile on her face so fake, it verged on deranged. "Well, isn't that lovely, Kit?"

Dad got up and pulled his suitcase over to the table. "C'mon, Iggy," he said, "let's have a drink." He popped open the lid and revealed his very own traveling liquor store, bottles and bottles of booze nestled in a very sparse collection of clothes.

"They have liquor stores in St. John's, you know," I said.

Dad ignored me and surveyed his stash. "What are you drinking these days, Ig? What can I get ya? We'll have a drink together—just like the old days."

Uncle Iggy stared into his teacup. "Well, you see, Phonse, the thing is, I've been going to these AA meeting thingies…"

"AA?" asked Dad.

"Yeah. You know, Alcoholics Anonymous?"

"I know what it is, Iggy. I just don't know why you'd want to go there."

Uncle Iggy rubbed his face with his hands. "I did something stupid."

"What?" asked Mom.

"I almost burned the house down."

Mom went pale. "What? What happened?"

Uncle Iggy ran his hands through his hair. "I was drunk. I don't know what happened. I…I…I don't know."

Mom reached out and took his hand. "It's okay, Iggy."

"I woke up and the house was filled with smoke."

That explained the smoky walls and ceilings.

"I must have dropped a lit cigarette somewhere."

His voice was going all cracked, and I prayed he wouldn't cry.

"The old man next door, Mr. Adams, he came in and woke me. The fire alarm was going off and I didn't even hear it. That's how out of it I was. The carpet was burning. I'm lucky it didn't spread. But then again, maybe…maybe…"

"No, Iggy," Mom said, staring him in the eye. "Don't even go there."

Go where? I was confused.

"Maybe I'd be better off if the whole place had blown up. With me in it." He dropped his head on the table and broke down. My stomach twisted into a tangled knot.

My mother hugged her brother tight. "Why didn't you tell us things were this bad? I knew you were a bit depressed, but—"

"I didn't want to talk about it," Uncle Iggy sobbed.

The room fell silent except for a few sniffles from Uncle Iggy and some *shhhs* from my mother. Then we heard the *kish* of a can being opened.

"Phonse!" yelled Mom.

"I need a friggin' drink after all of that," said Dad, guzzling a beer. "That's some heavy stuff."

Uncle Iggy stared hard at my father. "Phonse, when I almost burned this place down I knew it was time to admit I was an alcoholic. What is it going to take before you do the same?"

My mother stood up and rubbed her hands together nervously. "Now, then, how about a nice cup of tea?"

"Why would I admit I was an alcoholic," asked Dad, "when I'm not?"

"It's milk and one sugar, right, Iggy?"

"Come with me, Phonse," said Iggy. "To AA. You can join me on my journey to sobriety."

My father burst out laughing. "Journey to friggin' sobriety?" He crushed the empty beer can against the table. "Is that the kind of bullshit this AA cult is telling ya? Friggin' AA. Taking the enjoyment out of people's lives, that's what they do. Who do they think they are, these AA people? I'll tell you who they are. I'll tell ya what AA stands for—arrogant arseholes."

Uncle Iggy looked over at me. "Why don't you watch your language and calm down, Phonse?"

Dad grabbed another can of beer from his suitcase and raised it in the air like it was a trophy. "This'll calm me down," he yelled. "This always calms me down. No one will ever tell me that I can't have the thing that calms me down!"

He opened the can and downed it. He was *soooo* far from calm.

Uncle Iggy pushed his chair back and stood up tall. He stared directly at my father. "If you want to drink, fine. It's your choice. But this is *my* house. So keep your voice down and watch your language in front of my sister and my niece."

Uncle Iggy didn't look so meek anymore.

Dad stared at him for a moment, then sat down. He opened a bottle of whiskey and poured himself a drink, eyeing Uncle Iggy the entire time.

Mom put her hands on her thighs and bent toward me until her face was in mine. "Why don't you go see your new room, Kit? Go on," she said. "Go check it out. That's a good girl."

Uncle Iggy put a hand on Mom's shoulder and pulled her away from me. "She's not a puppy, Emily."

Uncle Iggy got my suitcase from where I'd left it by the front door.

"Your room's upstairs," he said. "Second door on the right."

"Thanks," I said. Then I dragged my case up the stairs to poor old dead Aunt Margie's sewing room and wished I was back in Parsons Bay in a room that smelled of me.

THE SEWING ROOM walls were covered with dark wood paneling. The one window in the room was tiny. I threw my suitcase on the bed and took a sniff. Thankfully, the room didn't smell like much of anything.

There was a glass candy dish on top of the dresser. I thought of Ms. Bartlett and Turkish delight. I took some change out of my pocket and threw it in the dish. One dollar and fifty cents. Not only was my new room a dark cave, but I was also poor.

Uncle Iggy poked his head in. "I put some of Margie's things in here," he said. "Some clothes and stuff. Help yourself. I have no use for any of it."

"Oh, okay, thanks."

After Uncle Iggy had left, I looked in the closet. Margie had good taste. I pulled on a denim jacket but felt weird wearing something that had belonged to someone else. Someone I had hardly known. Someone who was dead. I hung it back up and shut the closet door.

Feeling claustrophobic, I went outside and sat on the porch. The iron railing was rusty, and the concrete steps were crumbling. The garden was a bunch of overgrown bushes and weeds, dotted here and there with chip wrappers and other scraps of paper. It was like there had been a windstorm on garbage day and no one had bothered to clean up afterward. What a shithole. My eyes wandered away from Uncle Iggy's house, and I took in the houses around me. I realized that this little shithole, my new home, was just one of many small shitholes in this giant shithole neighborhood. I wondered how far from Uncle Iggy's house I'd have to walk before the atmosphere changed to something nicer.

I thought about Nan's kitchen. I thought about sitting at her table, drinking baby tea, listening to her transistor radio and watching the fishing boats coming back to port, knowing they had a full catch by the swarm of gulls around them. I was nestled deep in my thoughts when something came flying toward me, jarring me back to my shithole existence. "Tally-ho!" someone yelled. I shielded my head with my arms and held my breath. Something bounced off my foot. I looked down. There in the dirt lay a big hunk of doughy-looking bread.

"What the hell?" I yelled.

"Eh-up, lass!"

I followed the voice and saw an old man in a brown cardigan standing on the steps of the house next door.

"What?"

"Eh-up, lass!"

"What?"

The old man let out an exaggerated sigh. "Don't you understand English? HELLO THERE, GIRL!"

"Oh, hi."

"Crackin' good day, eh?" He swept his arms up toward the sky.

I looked at the overcast sky above me.

"Um, I guess so."

He started to sing. "'*Oh what a beautiful mornin', oh, what a beautiful day. I've got a beautiful feelin', everything's goin' my way.*'"

He looked at me expectantly, as if I was supposed to say something. But what do you say after someone sings? I wondered if I should clap. Maybe he was expecting me to break out in song. Maybe he wanted to do a duet. Maybe he lived his life as a musical.

"Um, nice song."

"Nice? Nice?" He made a combination of exasperated noises—*harrumph, tsk-tsk, tut-tut*—and started to walk back into his house.

"Hey," I called, picking up the lump of bread. "What's this?"

"What's *that*? I'll 'ave you know that *that* is a Yorkshire pudding. Been 'round for a donkey's age. From way back in the Middle Ages, like."

"Interesting," I said. "But why did you throw it at me?"

He looked at me as if the answer was obvious. "Flippin' hell! It's a welcome present, lass. Serve it with roast beef and gravy! Ta-ra!"

He went back into his house and left me on Uncle Iggy's front step. I put the Yorkshire pudding to my nose and took a whiff. It actually smelled quite good—good enough to eat…except for the grass and gravel.

I went inside and told Uncle Iggy what had happened. "Look what the guy next door threw at me," I said, holding up the Yorkshire pudding.

Uncle Iggy laughed. "Typical Mr. Adams."

"Mr. Adams? The guy who saved you from the fire?"

"Yep. If it wasn't for him, I wouldn't be here right now. Strange old guy. Harmless enough though."

I threw the hunk of dough into the garbage. Imagine throwing a Yorkshire pudding at someone. Still, I was relieved that he hadn't thrown a side of roast beef as well.

LIVING WITH THREE jobless adults wasn't easy. I never got a moment alone in the house, so I spent most of the summer sitting on the front step. I didn't mind though; it was my very own thinking spot.

"Come in, Kit," Uncle Iggy said, one cool August night. "It's getting chilly. Come watch *The Cosby Show* with us."

"No, thanks," I said. "I can hear Dad imitating Bill Cosby from here. His impersonation sucks. And anyway, they're reruns. I've seen them all before."

Uncle Iggy sat next to me. "You can't sit out here all the time, Kit."

"Why not?"

"Because I don't think it's good to be alone all the time."

"You're alone all the time," I said. "You barely leave your room."

"That's different."

"How?"

"Because at your age you should be, I dunno, hanging out with friends."

I laughed. "What friends? I don't have any here."

"Well, you will. School starts soon, right? That's something to be excited about."

"Woohoo."

"Look, Kit, I know how you feel. Believe me, I had to drag myself out of my room tonight. But now that you guys are living here, maybe we should, I dunno, start having some family time."

I pushed some crumbling concrete off the step with my heel. "I don't spend time with my family. It always ends in disaster. And I'm not going to waste my evenings watching *him* get drunk while Mom pretends everything is perfectly normal. So you can get the 'happy family' idea out of your head. It's not going to happen. What I need is space and peace and quiet, not family time."

Uncle Iggy got up. "Follow me."

"I'm not going," I said. "The last thing I want to do is listen to that lunatic yell at the TV."

He sighed. "Just follow me, Kit."

Inside, he opened the door to his den. "It's all yours."

"What?"

"My den. Privacy *and* warmth. Consider it yours."

"Really?"

"Really."

Like almost every other room in the house, the wood-paneled den was drab and dark. But I didn't care. It was way bigger than Aunt Margie's sewing room. It had a TV and a desk, and now it was mine. I threw my arms around Uncle Iggy. At first he didn't hug back. It was like he'd forgotten how. But then he smiled and returned the hug.

Uncle Iggy's university diplomas hung on the wall. A Bachelor of Science in Ocean and Naval Architectural Engineering hung next to a Master of Science in the same thing. When Mom would brag about how well Uncle Iggy was doing at university, Dad would dismiss it. "Ocean and Naval Arch-a-whatever-the-hell-they-call-it, my arse. Shipbuilding is what it is. Men have been building ships and boats for years and years, and they never needed no fancy university degree to do it either."

"You were at university for a long time," I said to Iggy now, studying the dates on the diplomas.

"Seven years in all," he said. "Seven wasted years."

He sat down on the loveseat.

"What happened?" I asked.

"Booze happened," he said. "After Margie died, I started drinking every night after work. Then eventually

I started drinking during the day. I kept a flask in my desk. It eased the pain at the time. But it was just a Band-Aid. Once the drink wore off, it was still there—the hurt, the grief."

"It must have been hard."

"It was. Still is."

"How did you lose your job?"

"The vessel designs I was turning in were far from seaworthy—they looked like doodles from a seven-year-old. They really had no choice but to fire me."

"But you stopped drinking. Won't they take you back now?"

"I had my chance, Kit, and I wrecked it. They won't trust me now."

"How about another company?"

"They'd want references that I'd never get. It's a lost cause."

I didn't know what to say.

"Don't ever start drinking, Kit."

"I'm proud of you for quitting," I said.

"Thanks, Kit."

MS. BARTLETT PUT in a good word with her family and got Mom a job at Bartlett's department store. Mom's first day of work coincided with Uncle Iggy's six-month anniversary of giving up alcohol. To celebrate, she planned a steak dinner.

"It's a special day," she said. "Iggy hasn't touched a drop in six months."

"Well, whoopdi-bloody-doo!" Dad exclaimed.

Mom ignored him. "So I went up to the butcher shop today and got some nice steak."

"Waste of bloody money," muttered Dad.

Mom flipped out. "I have a job now and will spend *my* money how *I* like. So until you get off your fat arse and get a job, you can keep your big trap shut about how I spend *my* earnings!"

I held my breath and looked at Dad. He was about to say something, but Mom cut him off.

"Kit, I'm making raisin buns for dessert and I need half a cup of butter. Run next door and see if whatsisname has any."

"Mom, I am NOT going over there! This isn't Parsons Bay, you know. This isn't like running down to Nan's. Mr. Adams is weird. He threw a Yorkshire pudding at me."

"I'm sure he's a lovely man. Now hurry up."

I went to the front door and hesitated.

"For the love of God, Kit, I'm sure he's not an axe murderer. Now get going!"

I walked up the path to Mr. Adams's front step. There was a sign posted in his flower bed: *Welcome to*

Yorkshire Cottage. It was a lovely sign, with beautiful gold lettering and green stenciled ivy. I guess Mr. Adams didn't think it was sufficient, though, because he had tacked on a paper sign underneath, written in what looked like felt pen. It read:

> *Hereby named God's Own County:*
> *Yorkshire,*
> *The best place on earth,*
> *Home of the world's second smallest mammal:*
> *the pygmy shrew*

This guy was a freak. Imagine being proud that your homeland was also home to a tiny shrew. I dreaded having to ask Mr. Adams for butter. What if he threw it at me like he had the Yorkshire pudding? I thought about running down to the store and buying the butter myself. But there was no time to escape. The front door opened. Before I could say anything, Mr. Adams spoke. "Come," he commanded. He said it so forcefully, I obeyed.

Mr. Adams's house was surprisingly bright and cheery, compared to Uncle Iggy's drab, dark dungeon. The living room was pretty, with a floral sofa and matching loveseat and duck-egg-blue walls that peeked out from a sea of framed photographs.

We walked through to the kitchen, which was sunshine yellow with matching yellow placemats on the table.

"Now then, how 'bout a nice cup o' tea, eh?"

"Well, actually…"

"I don't often 'ave visitors."

"I, uh…"

"I've got some lovely bickies here somewhere," he said, raking through a cupboard.

"Actually—" I said again, but I was cut off when Mr. Adams, hearing a lawn mower suddenly start up across the street, jumped to the window, shook his head in disgust and said, "Ee by gum! There's nought as queer as folk."

"What?"

"I said, *Ee by gum! There's nought as queer as folk.*"

"I heard you, I just didn't understand you."

Mr. Adams rolled his eyes and spoke slowly. "Oh my God. There is nothing as strange as people."

I joined him at the window and watched one of his neighbors mowing his lawn.

"He's just mowing his lawn," I said.

"Aye, but on a day like today?" he said, his face distorted as if he were an actor being terrorized in a horror movie.

I looked into the sky. "It's a nice, sunny day."

"Exactly! And that daft bugger is ruining it with that horrible noise. He's gormless, I say, gormless!"

Mr. Adams seemed to think everyone around him was crazy and he was perfectly sane. Maybe he was right. I was sick of normal people anyway. Maybe they're the crazy ones after all.

"What's gormless?" I asked.

Mr. Adams frowned at me. "You must be gormless to 'ave to ask what's gormless."

I thought for a moment. "Does it mean stupid?"

Mr. Adams stuck his pointer finger in the air. "Ding, ding, ding. We 'ave a winner!"

"Do you really need to be so sarcastic?" I grumbled.

He rubbed his chin and thought for a moment. "Aye, aye, I do."

Unbelievable.

He started rooting through the cupboard again. "Now where are my Jammy Dodgers?" "

"Your what?" I asked.

He whipped his head around so fast, he hit his head on the cupboard door. "Bloody hell, me poor head!" he yelled. "Don't you know owt?"

"Owt?"

He sighed. "Owt means anything and a Jammy Dodger is a bloody bickie. You know what a bickie is, don't you?"

"A biscuit. Although, personally, I'd call it a cookie."

Mr. Adams snorted. "Cookie. What a daft word."

"Daft?"

"'Ave I got to explain everything to you? Daft! Barmy! Stupid!"

I shrugged. "I don't understand your language."

"My language is bloody English!"

"Could've fooled me," I muttered.

Mr. Adams looked angry and amused at the same time. "You're a right cheeky little bugger, aren't you?"

I laughed. "Yeah, I guess I am."

He kind of smiled, then turned away. "Now then, how 'bout that tea?"

I had to tell him I needed to borrow butter, but I really wanted to stay and have tea. There was something about the kitchen that was comforting. Something familiar. But I had to get back home. Mom would have a fit if she couldn't finish her buns in time for supper.

"Well, actually, I just came to borrow some butter. A half cup…my mother needs it for some raisin buns."

His face fell. "Oh, aye. Butter." He pulled a block of butter out of the fridge and handed it to me.

Before I left, I turned to him. "Did you save my uncle?"

"Eh? Save? What are you on about, lass?"

"The fire. Uncle Iggy said a neighbor woke him up."

"Oh, aye. At first I thought it were a giant weenie roast or something. But then I heard the alarm going off. He's a heavy sleeper, your uncle."

A heavy drinker, I thought.

"Well, thanks," I said. "For that, and for the butter."

He nodded. "What's your name, lass?"

"Kit. Kit Ryan."

"Kit-Kit Ryan?"

"No, just Kit."

"I'm Reginald Adams."

"Bye, Mr. Adams."

"Ta-ra, love."

"Where on earth have you been?" Mom asked when I got home.

"I got stuck talking to Mr. Adams next door," I said. "I couldn't get away from him. That old geezer's a nutcase." I felt a pang of guilt the moment I said it.

"Well, I hope you used your manners and said thank you," said Mom.

I couldn't shake the look of disappointment on Mr. Adams's face when I told him I'd just come for butter.

"Kit, are you listening to me?"

"What?"

My mother shook her head and sighed. "Make yourself useful and go tell Iggy supper will be ready in about twenty minutes."

I went upstairs and knocked on his bedroom door. I took the grunt I heard as a "come in." When I entered, I could barely see Iggy through the haze of cigarette smoke. He was sitting on an old wooden chair, staring out the window. As soon as I saw him, I felt another pang of guilt. I should have said yes to family time the other night. Poor Iggy had made an effort, and all I'd done was shoot him down. I'd pushed him back into his shell.

I looked around. His bed was unmade, and on every surface there was a full ashtray. I went downstairs and returned with a plastic bag. Then I threw open the window and dumped all the cigarette butts into the bag.

"You don't have to do that, Kit."

"Someone has to," I said. "This place is a mess. And you're a mess too. Just look at you. What happened to all your nice clothes?"

Uncle Iggy stubbed out his cigarette. "Nice clothes, nice house...none of that matters anymore."

I sat on the edge of the bed. "You make me sad, Uncle Iggy."

He turned around, startled. "Oh, Kit. Just ignore me, please. I'll be okay. It's just hard to feel happy all the time."

"Mom's made a special dinner. Because you haven't had a drink in six months. That's something to be happy about, isn't it?"

He gave a little laugh. "Yes, I suppose it is."

I stood up. "So come on. Let's go eat."

"I'll be down in a minute," he said, "after I change into something decent."

I smiled. "Good. Because I'm sick of looking at those old sweatpants."

He laughed. "Me too."

I was almost out the door when he said, "One day at a time, hey, Kit?"

I turned around. "Yep. One day at a time."

THREE
Slacks

Bartlett's was the fanciest department store in St. John's. But it wasn't cool. It was where old people shopped. And now, armed with her evil staff discount, Mom claimed it was the best place to buy new school clothes.

"I don't want to go shopping," I groaned.

"Oh, go on," Uncle Iggy said. "It'll be fun." He looked at Mom. "You two should make the day of it. Go out for lunch."

"Oh, I don't have time for that," Mom said. "I have a few groceries to get today and supper won't make itself, you know."

"Why don't you just give me the money?" I suggested. "I can pick out new clothes by myself, like I always do."

"Because I need to be there," she said. "To get the discount."

We took the bus downtown in silence.

"Look at all the back-to-school shoppers," said Mom as we weaved our way through the crowds in Bartlett's.

I looked around. Everyone I saw was middle-aged or older.

"These are lovely," she said, picking up a pair of puke-green polyester pants with an elasticized waist.

"They're wonderful."

"Come on now, Kit. Don't be sarcastic. These are a fine pair of slacks."

"Slacks. Enough said."

"And look," she said, picking up a yellow and green cardigan, "this will match perfectly."

"I'll look like a giant booger."

"Kit, don't be disgusting. At least try them on."

"Mom," I moaned, "they're for old ladies. I don't need an elastic waist!"

She sighed. "Okay, let's keep looking."

The Junior Fashions department at Bartlett's was horrible. I don't even know how they got away with the word *fashion*…there was nothing fashionable in sight.

I suggested the Denim Den at the mall, but Mom said, "There's just not enough selection in those small stores," which was her way of saying we couldn't afford it.

"Besides," she added, "it'd be a shame to waste my staff discount."

I knew I would never win the clothes war with Mom, especially with her new secret weapon, so I eventually settled on a plain red sweater, a striped shirt, a blue hoodie, some brown cords and a pair of boring blue jeans that sat too high on my waist. Far from cool.

Uncle Iggy looked apologetic when we got home. Dad was plastered.

"I tried talking sense into him," he said. "But the more I told him he'd had enough, the more he drank."

"Kitty! Kitster! The Kit-en-ator!" Dad boomed from his chair. "Give us a fashion parade!"

"A fashion parade?" I said. "With what I got today? It'll be the fastest parade in history."

"Oh, c'mon, Itty-Bitty-Kitty," said Dad. "Lemme see your new duds."

I scowled at him. "Duds?"

"I don't think she wants to try anything on right now," said Uncle Iggy.

But my father wouldn't drop it. "C'mon now, Kitty. Let's see how beautiful you'll look."

I stormed over to where my father sat, stood over him and yelled, "Beautiful? I have one pair of ugly jeans, three boring tops and a pair of shit-brown cords. That's it! I wasn't out buying a bloody prom dress or anything!"

Uncle Iggy gave me a warning look. "Kit, why don't you take your stuff upstairs?"

My father caught Iggy's look and said, "She's not going anywhere. I *paid* for the clothes, so I should bloody well be able to see them."

"Actually," I said, "Mom paid for them. You don't have a job, remember? But you want to see them? Sure! Here! Have a look!"

I raised the Bartlett's bag over my head and threw it, hard, right into my dad's gut.

"Kit!" my mother yelled.

Uncle Iggy quickly moved in front of me, blocking me from Dad. But Dad just sat there quietly and when he spoke, his voice was careful and calm.

"You know what, Emily?" he said. "We should have said yes. We should have left the ungrateful little brat back in Parsons Bay."

The room fell silent.

"Mom? What's he talking about?"

She looked away.

Iggy spoke to my dad through gritted teeth. "Don't ever talk to her like that again."

Dad ignored him. He said, "Did you hear me, Emily? Did you hear what I said? We should have said yes to that hippie-dippie freak show while we had the chance."

"What's going on, Emily?" Uncle Iggy said. "What's he talking about?"

"Go ahead. Tell 'em, Emily," said Dad, his voice tinged with spite.

Mom's voice was low. "Ms. Bartlett offered to take you in, Kit. While me and your father came to St. John's to find work."

My head was spinning.

"She did?"

My mother nodded.

"And you said no?"

She nodded again.

"Why? Why did you say no?" I yelled. "You knew I didn't want to leave!"

"Because you're our responsibility, Kit, not Ms. Bartlett's. You belong here. With us."

"I don't belong here. I hate it here. I hate being away from Nan and I hate having to go to a new school and I'd give anything not to have to live with my asshole father!"

"What the hell did you call me?" Dad roared. He jumped up from his chair and lunged forward. Uncle Iggy grabbed his shoulders and held him back.

I screamed at my mother, "You should have told me that Ms. Bartlett offered to take me in! At least then I'd know that *someone* has my best interests at heart, that *someone* gives a rat's ass about me!"

"We *all* care about you!" my mother cried.

I pointed at my father. Iggy was still holding him back from doing God knows what. "You call that caring, Mom?"

She looked crushed. "Kit, please…"

I walked out the door and slammed it behind me.

Mr. Adams was in his garden. I was too mad to ask what he was doing, but it looked like he was shaping one of his bushes to look like Elmo.

"Take a deep breath, flower," he said. "Why don't you go for a walk and blow off some steam? There's a nice park down the road. 'Bout one mile past Pelley's Pharmacy."

Flower. I liked that. Better than *ungrateful little brat.*

I sat in the park for an hour. It was cold. It was damp. And it was boring. So I went back home, took the pitiful $1.50 out of poor old dead Aunt Margie's candy dish and went to Pelley's.

"I BOUGHT SOME bickies," I said when Mr. Adams opened his door.

He sighed as if I was causing him a great inconvenience.

"I suppose I'll 'ave to put the kettle on."

"I suppose you will."

The hint of a smile appeared on his face.

I passed him the gingersnaps I'd bought. "I couldn't find Jammy Dodgers."

"That's because I get 'em specially ordered. Imported, like. From Bartlett's."

I slumped in a chair at the kitchen table. "I might be able to get you a discount then," I said flatly. "My mother works there."

His face lit up. "Really? A penny saved is a penny gained!"

I didn't smile back.

"Somethin' wrong, lass? You've got a face like a slapped arse."

This time, I smiled back.

"Whatever it is, flower, a cuppa will help."

He placed a pot of tea on the table and covered it in a multicolored crocheted tea cozy.

"Nice," I said.

"The missus made it. Before she died, of course."

"Of course."

"Did you know," he said, "that the longest street name in York is Whip-Ma-Whop-Ma-Gate?"

"Cool."

We sipped our tea without speaking. And that was when I realized what was so familiar, so comforting, about Mr. Adams's kitchen. It was the radio. I hadn't put my finger on it the day I came to borrow butter, but sure enough, there it was—the soft murmur in the background. I followed the sound and saw a little transistor sitting on the windowsill, just like at Nan's. And the walls. The walls were yellow. All I needed now was for Mr. Adams to put on an apron and start baking bread. I looked down to hide the smirk that had appeared on my face.

"Are you laughin' at my skirtin' boards?"

"Your what?"

"My skirtin' boards. You must know what skirtin' boards are! What the bloody hell are they teachin' at school these days?"

"The usual. English, math, science."

Mr. Adams made a noise that sounded like a cross between *harrumph* and *pshaw* and, for added effect, threw his hands up in the air as he said it.

I helped myself to a biscuit.

"They're dusty," he said.

I looked at the biscuits. "They are? How did they get dusty?"

I didn't understand—we had just opened them.

He looked at me like I was an idiot. "I can't get down on the floor to clean 'em, *that's* how they got dusty. A man my age can't be bent over cleanin' skirtin' boards. My poor ol' back can't take it. I'd get stuck in a bent-over position forever."

Oh, the skirting boards.

"I can't keep 'em spick-and-span like Elspeth used to," he said.

"Was she your maid?"

"Nay. My wife."

"Oh."

"She died ten years ago."

"I'm sorry."

He nodded.

"How did you and Elspeth meet?"

"She were on holiday in Yorkshire and—"

"Oh, yeah," I interrupted. "Home of the pygmy shrew."

Mr. Adams's face lit up. "Ee by gum!" He beamed. "How'd you know?"

"It's on the sign in front of your house."

Mr. Adams frowned. "Aye," he grumbled. "Well, at least you can read. Anyhoo, Elspeth was on holiday in Yorkshire and her family's old Morris Minor broke down right in front of my family's sheep farm. I went to the rescue, Elspeth and I locked eyes, and the rest were history. In a nutshell, I left the farm, moved to Sheffield, where she was from, and got meself a job at the steel factory. That were the big industry in Sheffield. Look," he said, grabbing a knife out of the drawer and waving it dangerously in my face. "I probably made that."

The words on the side of the knife said *Made in Sheffield.*

"Ee, there's a crackin' knife," he said, gazing at it. "They don't make 'em like they used to. Just look at the craftsmanship."

"So," I said, "it was love at first sight?"

"Are you bloody crackers? I said it was a crackin' knife. I didn't say I were in bloody love with it. Do you think I'm daft or something?"

"I was talking about Elspeth."

"Oh, Elspeth. Aye. It were love at first sight. Her mother didn't like it, not one bit. She wanted more for her daughter than an ex-sheep-farmin' steelworker. But that didn't stop Elspeth and me from gettin' together on the sly, meetin' in private, like. She were bonny, my Elspeth. From the moment I met her till the day she died, she were a bonny lass."

I wanted to hear more, and I was starting to think that maybe he wasn't so crazy after all when he started talking to the sugar.

"C'mon, little sugary," he said, "into the tea you go, little fella."

"Tell me more about Elspeth. Were you ever caught together? How did you get married—did you elope?"

"Bloody heck, lass! You're not backward at coming forward, are you?"

"Huh?"

"Nosy is what you are. And idle too. Sittin' here all day eatin' my bickies. G'on! Shift yourself! Out with you!"

I got up to leave.

"You 'aven't finished your tea," he said. "Maybe you could come back and finish it another time. I'll make a fresh cup, like."

"Okay," I said. I was on my way out the door when an idea popped into my head.

"Mr. Adams?"

"Aye?"

"How about I do a bit of cleaning for you? You know, keep your skirting boards spick-and-span? Once a week, maybe?"

Mr. Adams grunted. "I suppose you'd want payin' for that."

I shrugged. "That's not why I suggested it. I was thinking more of your poor ol' back. I wouldn't want you walking around like a hunchback."

"Well, I'll need time to think about it," he snapped. "You can't just spring that on someone and expect an answer straightaway."

I was barely off his property when I heard his side window open.

"Five dollars a week," he called, "and you'd better do a good job."

Five dollars. What a cheapskate. Still, I probably would've done it for free just to escape the madness of home.

WHEN I GOT back from Mr. Adams's house, Mom said she was sorry. For not telling me about Ms. Bartlett's offer, for not letting me have a say in it.

But her apology turned into a lecture. "There was no need of throwing a bag at your father like that. We have to play the cards we've been dealt. We don't have a lot of money for fancy clothes and that's that. There's no point in complaining about it."

She went on and on and on...telling me I must be positive...telling me I shouldn't be so negative...blah, blah, blah. Eventually she ended with, "Now I'll say no more about it," which was just as well because there wasn't much else to be said.

I went to my den, and a moment later there was a knock on the door.

"Can I come in?" I heard Iggy say.

"I guess."

He opened the door and stood in the doorway. "I know things are hard right now, Kit, but they will get better. You can carve out your own little life in this world. Keep going to school, go to university, make your own happiness. Don't get caught up in the unhappiness around you. Move on. Stay strong."

"Excuse me? *You* are telling *me* to 'make my own happiness'? To 'move on'? Perhaps you should take your own advice and get on with *your* life. Sitting in this depressing shithole all day long, smoking up a storm, won't bring her back, you know!"

Uncle Iggy looked like I'd just punched him in the stomach.

I rushed past him and ran to my room.

That night I tossed and turned. Three words marched through my head like enemy soldiers overtaking my thoughts. They charged this way and that, pounding out a harsh, horrible little rhythm as they went. *Ungrateful little brat, ungrateful little brat.* I sat up suddenly and switched on the light, hoping to blind them away. I shook my head, even smacked it with my hand, trying to loosen their tight lock on my mind. I turned out the light and tried to find sleep. *Ungrateful little brat, ungrateful little brat.* I gave up and went downstairs. Nan said warm milk always did the trick for her. I grabbed the *Shop 'Til You Drop* memo pad that was stuck to the fridge and, while my milk warmed in the microwave, wrote a letter to Anne-Marie. I wrote about Dad being a jerk and the Bartlett's clothes and Mom's stupid discount. I wrote about how Uncle Iggy had changed and how weird, in a good way, Mr. Adams was and how nervous I was about school starting the next day. I wrote and wrote and wrote, until I'd reached the cardboard sheet at the bottom of the pad.

When I went back to bed, I felt a thousand pounds lighter. The noise in my head was gone, and my breathing was steady and even. I pulled the covers up to my chin and snuggled deep inside them, hiding from the autumn chill that crept though Uncle Iggy's drafty house. As I dozed off I thought about asking Mom to pick me up some looseleaf paper from Bartlett's, in case I wanted to write again. Then I fell into a dream where I was on top of the cliff in Parsons Bay, wearing the green polyester pants and green and yellow V-neck from Bartlett's. Dad was there, and he was laughing at me. He called me a giant snot. I took out the folded pages of the *Shop Til You Drop* memo pad from my back pocket and read him the letter I'd written to Anne-Marie. He stopped laughing. Satisfied, I stood at the cliff's edge and let the salt air blow over my face. I licked my lips and smiled.

I HAD JUST changed into my hideous Bartlett's clothes when Mom knocked on my door.

I opened up. "Yeah?"

"I have something for you."

She handed me a Denim Den bag.

"For your first day of school. Have a look."

I reached in and pulled out a pair of new jeans and an oversized sweater.

"I hope you like them."

They looked perfect.

"Do you think they'll fit?" she asked.

All I could do was nod.

"Well, you'd better get a move on. Don't want to be late on your first day."

My mother started down the stairs. I felt like running after her, grabbing hold of her and hugging her tight, but all I managed was a squeaky thank-you before she got out of earshot.

I changed into my new clothes and, feeling like a new and improved Kit Ryan, headed off for school.

At the bottom of Mr. Adams's walkway was a box marked *free to a good home*. I peered into it, half expecting to see a litter of kittens or puppies. I say *half* expected because I was learning that with Mr. Adams, you should expect the unexpected...and kittens and puppies would make too much sense.

The half of me that expected the unexpected was right. Inside the box was a single necktie in an aardvark print. I made a mental note to look in the box on the way home.

My new high school was huge. A big brick two-story building, it was a far cry from the little wooden one back home. It looked more like a prison than a school. The student population—all girls—was one thousand— the same as the entire population of Parsons Bay. I felt like a teeny tiny fish in a humongous pond.

A prissy-looking girl stood behind a registration table. Her shoulder-length hair was cut in layers; blond highlights framed her perfectly made-up face. "Name?" she said.

I ran my fingers through my hair, as if that would help it look better.

"Kit Ryan."

She looked me up and down with a slight wrinkle in her nose, like there was a bad smell somewhere. It was a good thing I wasn't wearing the Bartlett's clothes or she might actually have vomited. She was wearing designer clothes. I couldn't say exactly what they were—stuff like that didn't exist in Parsons Bay—but they looked expensive. Her plaid miniskirt and polo shirt with the little embroidered alligator were not my style. I imagined us having a vomit-off over whose clothes were worse. She checked her list, then passed me a map. "Room two oh six," she said. I glanced at her boobs. I couldn't help it. They were huge.

"Jealous?" she asked, looking down at her chest.

I snatched the map. "Far from it."

The map was useless. I got lost trying to find the stairs to the second floor. I went through a door at the end of a long hallway, hoping to find the stairwell, and ended up outside in a courtyard full of picnic tables instead. A curly-haired boy stood in the corner.

"*Vous êtes perdu?*"

"What?"

"Are you lost?"

"Why are you speaking French?"

"I'm impressed." His smile was big and dimpled and cocky.

"With what?" I asked.

"You recognized the language."

"Yeah, look, sorry to be rude, but I have to go. I'm trying to find the stairs to the second floor."

He laughed. "Well, they're not out here."

I felt my face turn red. "Obviously not."

"Oooh, touchy," he said. "First-day jitters?"

I looked at my watch. Five to nine. "I just need to get to my class," I snapped. "I'm going to be late."

As I turned to go inside, I tripped on a banana peel. Seriously. A banana peel. I'd only ever seen that on Saturday-morning cartoons. Somehow, on my first day of school, with a cute boy watching, I'd managed to make a complete fool out of myself. And it wasn't just a little stumble either. I actually tripped on the stupid thing, lost my balance and was vaulted toward the door. With no time to put my hands out to break my fall, I quickly twisted my body to the side (to save my face) and smashed the left side of my body into the door.

"Aw, geez," I muttered through gritted teeth. I grasped my left arm and shoulder and slid down the door, coming to rest at the bottom. "I'm such an idiot!"

"You said it," said the boy.

"You're really annoying, do you know that?" I growled.

He laughed and walked toward me.

"Here," he said, reaching out his hand. "*Laisse-moi t'aider.*"

"I don't know what that means." I groaned. "And I don't care."

"I said, Let me help."

"Um, I don't think so. I can manage, thank you very much."

He held up his hands. "Okeydokey. It's your funeral."

I knew using my left hand to push myself up off the ground would be impossible, so I leaned over and put my right hand down. I winced in pain. It seemed that any movement, however slight, made my left arm and shoulder throb. So I moved back to my original position. And winced again. I was stuck.

The boy put his hand out again.

"Don't touch me."

"You can't sit here all day."

"I don't have a choice. I can't move."

The bell rang. He grabbed my hand and tried to pull me up.

"Ouch!" I yelled. "Get your grubby hands off me, Moptop!"

He dropped my hands, folded his arms and stared at me. "Oh God. I am so sorry. It's just…your hair…it's…crazy." He raised his eyebrows.

"It's like a bird's nest or something."

He laughed. "Keep digging that hole." ·

"It's the pain," I said. "It's making me delirious."

He smiled and squatted down in front of me. He took my right arm and, slowly and carefully, laid it over his right shoulder. Then he wrapped his arm around my waist and in one swift movement pulled me up to standing. We were chest to chest. The pain disappeared. He smelled like fruity shampoo and Mentos.

"What's your name?" he whispered.

My stomach filled with butterflies. "Kit."

He leaned in closer, put his mouth close to my ear. "You okay, Kit?"

I pulled away. I didn't want him to feel how fast my heart was beating.

"I'm fine," I snapped, trying to keep my voice from shaking. "Don't you have a school to go to or something?"

"Yeah. The boys' school down the road. It starts fifteen minutes later than yours."

"So…what, you hang out here every morning just to annoy people?"

"No, I hang out here to see my girlfriend."

I felt a pang of disappointment.

He reached for the door. "Would you like me to hold this open so you can walk *through* it this time?"

"Very funny."

"Go back down the hall and take the second door on the left. You'll find the stairwell there."

"Thanks."

"*Au revoir, mon petit agneau perdu.*"

"Um, bye."

I could feel him watching me as I walked down the hall.

"By the way," he called. "I like the nickname."

I turned around. "What?"

"The nickname. Moptop. I like it."

"Oh…well…you're welcome, I guess."

He laughed and let go of the door. I waited a moment, and as soon as I heard the door click shut, I leaned against the wall and caught my breath. As my heartbeat slowed and the warmth in my chest faded away, the pain came back. And I stood in the empty hallway and cried.

BY THE TIME I'd pulled myself together, I was forty-five minutes late for class. Everyone stared at me.

"Didn't I tell you your room number, like, five hours ago?" It was Miss Priss from the gym. She was sitting in the front row.

Mr. Byrne, the homeroom teacher, gave her a sharp look. "New students are bound to get lost, Ms. Shea. It's perfectly understandable."

I took an empty seat next to a girl wearing dark eye makeup and a Nirvana T-shirt. "Don't mind Amanda," she whispered. "In case you haven't noticed, she's the school bitch."

Mr. Byrne introduced me to the class as the "new girl from Parsons Bay."

Amanda turned around and looked at me. "Oh, you're from the bay. No wonder you got lost. This school is probably as big as your whole town."

"My town's not *that* small," I lied. "I mean, it's not as big as St. John's, but—"

She cut me off. "Oh, your accent," she said. "It's so… different."

There were a few giggles.

"Ignore her," the girl next to me whispered.

Mr. Byrne passed me a textbook. Without thinking, I reached for it with my left hand, and as soon as he let go, I dropped it and yelped in pain.

"What's wrong?" he asked.

"I, uh, had a bit of an accident on the way here."

He looked concerned. "What kind of accident?"

All eyes were on me. I felt myself blush. "I tripped and fell."

"Let me see." Mr. Byrne reached over and gently moved my arm.

"Aw, sweet Jesus!" I screamed.

The class erupted in laughter.

"Are you left- or right-handed?" he asked.

"Right."

"You're lucky…I don't think you'll be using that left arm for a while."

"Great," I muttered.

"You need to get this looked at right away," he said. "I'll call your parents."

UNCLE IGGY TOOK me to the hospital. Mom was working, and Dad would have risked a DUI if he got behind the wheel.

Watching Uncle Iggy deal with an emergency was hysterical, even though I was in pain. He was *so* out of his comfort zone. He could barely concentrate on driving, and once we got to the hospital he paced the floors of the ER, asked the doctors a million questions and asked me if I was okay ten thousand times. He was so high-maintenance, the doctors asked if he'd like something for his nerves. When he said yes, they had to explain that they were joking. It turned out my collarbone was fractured, and I was going to have to wear a sling for six weeks.

Uncle Iggy bought me an ice-cream sundae at Dairy Queen on the way home.

"The last person who took me out for ice cream was you," I said. "You took me and Anne-Marie the last time you came to Parsons Bay, remember?"

"Yeah, I remember. Was that really the last time you went out for ice cream?"

"Yeah, but it's no big deal."

"It is a big deal. That was four years ago."

I scooped up a spoonful of hot fudge. "Yeah, well, Mom's busy and I wouldn't be caught dead out in public with Dad anyway."

"Do they ever take you anywhere? A restaurant? A movie?"

I didn't answer. I just looked down at my sundae.

Uncle Iggy shook his head and stared out the window. "Unbelievable," he muttered.

I tried to change the subject. "This sundae is really good. How's yours? I might try strawberry next time."

"I mean, who doesn't do stuff with their kids?" He didn't direct the question at me. He seemed to be asking his reflection, or some invisible person on the other side of the window. "Isn't it just second nature to take your kids out for ice cream or a hamburger or something?"

I rolled my eyes and flicked my hand in the air, as if I was swatting away Uncle Iggy's ridiculous ideas.

"I'm sixteen," I said. "I'm not a little kid. I don't care about stuff like that."

Uncle Iggy looked at me. "I bet you do."

"I bet I don't."

"I *know* you do," he challenged.

"How?"

"Because you said *next time*."

"Huh?"

"You said, *I might try strawberry next time.* So you do care. You're enjoying this and would like to do it again. Right?"

I shrugged and sucked in my lips to keep from smiling.

He moved in closer and raised his eyebrows. "Right?"

"Maybe," I said.

"How about we pick a night? Say, Wednesdays. And once a week we'll go out for supper or dessert or something. Sound good?"

I smiled. "Sounds good."

Satisfied, Uncle Iggy went back to his strawberry sundae.

"Hey," I said, mixing hot fudge into my melting ice cream, "your hair is messy."

Uncle Iggy frowned. "That's not very nice, Kit."

"No, I mean in a good way. Like, on purpose."

He reached up and touched his hair. "Well, I did use a bit of product this morning."

"It looks good."

"Thanks."

"Uncle Iggy?"

"Yeah?"

"You know that stuff about it being second nature to do stuff with your kids?"

"Yeah? What about it?"

"You're going to make a great father someday."

I didn't think there was such a thing as a sad smile, but that's what I saw on Uncle Iggy's face. "Thanks, Kit. But that dream died when Margie did."

"You might meet someone else someday. You never know."

He looked doubtful.

"One day at a time, hey, Uncle Iggy?"

He smiled again, and this time it was less sad.

"Yep, one day at a time."

After our sundaes we went home, but before going into the house I took the aardvark-patterned tie out of Mr Adams's *free to a good home* box.

As I went up the front path, I noticed the iron railing had a new coat of paint on it and the garden was cleared of all the garbage.

"You've been busy this morning, Uncle Iggy."

"Go look in your den."

The furniture was covered in plastic sheeting, and there were two gallons of paint on the floor. Uncle Iggy popped one of the lids off.

"I love it," I said. "It's almost identical to the yellow in Nan's kitchen."

"I was just getting started when the school called."

"Why are you doing this, Uncle Iggy? Your hair, the front garden. Why the change?"

"You were right," he said. "This place really is a shit-hole. Time to brighten things up a bit. And what better place to start than this dungeon? I didn't think you'd mind."

"Not at all," I said. "I just have one request."

"What's that?"

"The diplomas stay. They're kinda, well, an...inspiration to me."

Uncle Iggy smiled. "Then they stay."

THE SLING WAS a big pain in the arse. Getting dressed was the worst. I hated having to ask for help, but I had no choice. I called for Mom, and she came in and shut the door behind her.

"I just need my, um, bra hooked up."

"Oh, okay," she said. "I can do that. Sure. I'll just do this right up for you."

She lifted up the back of my shirt and, with freezing fingers, fastened my bra.

"Anything else?"

I needed my hair pulled back in a ponytail, but I shook my head.

She went out and shut the door behind her.

It was Dad's fault that Mom and I avoided all that mother-daughter stuff—the bra shopping, the girly lunches, the chick flicks. Whenever it was the two of us, there was too much unsaid stuff hanging around, like a dark cloud. So we just didn't bother.

I looked in the mirror and pulled a headband over my hair with one hand. It looked like crap. I grabbed my backpack and left my room, slamming the door behind me.

FOUR

The Drunk-O-Meter

My second day of school was marginally better than the first. I got lost again trying to find my homeroom. Luckily, the girl who'd sat next to me the day before saw me wandering aimlessly and took pity on me.

She pointed at my sling. "Broken?"

"Yep."

"Can you still write?"

"Yeah, why?" I asked.

She passed me a petition.

"It's to have a carpentry class started at our school," she said. "If the boys' school down the road can have shop class, why can't we?"

I thought of Anne-Marie and her paint-spattered overalls and immediately put my name down. I was the first one to sign it.

"Thanks," she said. "I'm Caroline, by the way."

"Kit," I said. "Kit Ryan."

She smiled. "Yeah, I know."

I looked at the clipboard. "Oh…right. I just wrote it down. Duh."

Caroline laughed. "Actually, I knew your name from yesterday. Mr. Byrne introduced you, remember?"

"Oh, yeah. I forgot. Yesterday was kind of a blur."

"Maybe you hit your head when you fell and got a concussion or something," Caroline said.

I laughed. "Maybe."

Caroline tugged on my good arm. "C'mon, we're gonna be late."

We wound our way through a series of long corridors and stairways and finally arrived at our classroom. Mr. Byrne frowned and glanced at the clock as we entered.

We put our heads down and walked quickly to our seats.

"Nice pants," Amanda Shea whispered as we passed her desk. "Corduroy is so…different. You're making quite the statement."

Caroline rolled her eyes. "I have a statement for you, Amanda." Then she said something I can't repeat. I almost choked laughing.

"Something funny you'd like to share, Kit?" asked Mr. Byrne.

I shook my head.

"Then let's get started." He pointed to a map of Newfoundland. "Today I'd like to talk about the rural parts of our province. Many of you would be surprised to know how differently people live on other parts of the island. Take a community like Cape St. George—many people there speak French. Accents and language vary from place to place."

Oh God, don't point me out, I thought. *Please don't point me out.*

Mr. Byrne wrote the letter *H* on the board. "How would you pronounce this, Kit?"

It was obvious. "Haitch."

The class roared with laughter. Amanda was practically doubled over. When she got control of herself, she raised her hand. "I guess fashion sense varies from place to place as well. Take Kit's pants, for example."

"That's quite enough, Ms. Shea," said Mr. Byrne. The sniggering died down and he moved on to unusual place names. Once he started listing towns from around the bay called Come By Chance, Spread Eagle, and Blow Me Down, everyone seemed to forget about my pants.

I was still fuming at lunchtime.

Caroline grabbed her lunch from her locker. "Don't let her get to you, Kit. She's not worth it."

I looked down at my pants. "I mean, are they really that bad?"

"She'll get bored, trust me."

"How can you be so sure?"

"Last year she started calling me Grunge-oline. I completely ignored her and eventually she stopped. She'll always be a bitch though. She can't help it. Must be in her DNA."

I looked at Caroline's ripped jeans and combat boots. Everyone in St. John's seemed to have a thing. Except me. I was just boring old mousy-haired, badly dressed Kit Ryan.

Caroline grabbed her leather jacket from her locker. "Wanna eat in the courtyard?"

"Sure, whatever."

"I can't stay long. Floor hockey starts in twenty minutes."

"Floor hockey? Really?"

Caroline laughed. "Surprised?"

I shrugged. "Kind of."

Caroline slammed her locker shut. "Don't worry, I don't play in my Doc Martens."

She looked at my empty hands. "Where's your lunch?"

The breadbox had been empty that morning, and the only thing in the fridge was leftover fishcakes, which I didn't dare take to school.

"I forgot it."

"You can share mine," said Caroline. "My mother packs me enough to feed an army."

We went outside and found an empty picnic table. Caroline gave me half of her turkey and Swiss sandwich.

"Thanks," I said, taking a bite.

The courtyard was packed with kids sitting in groups. I was glad I wasn't sitting on my own.

"I met a cute guy out here yesterday," I said, hoping to start a conversation that would make Caroline want to have lunch with me the next day and the day after that.

"Really?"

"Yeah. He was kind of charming but obnoxious at the same time."

Caroline's eyes lit up. "Charming and obnoxious? I'm intrigued. Tell me more."

So I told her the whole story—the French, the banana peel, the dimples, the fall, the embrace—and she enjoyed every minute of it. I was just getting to the Moptop part when Amanda burst into the courtyard.

"Aw, geez," I said. "Her again? I can't seem to get away from that girl."

"Hurry up," Amanda barked to some poor fool behind her.

"She's such a witch," said Caroline.

Amanda looked around the courtyard for a free table. The person she'd barked at came through the door and joined her.

"Oh God, that's him," I said.

The poor fool was Moptop.

"Oh, Kit." Caroline groaned. "That's Elliot Harris. Amanda's *boyfriend*!"

"Are you kidding me?"

"I kid you not."

"Ugh."

"Ugh is right," said Caroline.

"I have the worst luck," I said.

Amanda pointed at me and whispered something in Elliot's ear. He looked at me and winked. I looked away.

Amanda spoke loudly, obviously for my benefit. "And then I said, *Take Kit's pants, for example*. Isn't that hysterical, Elliot?"

I felt my face turn red.

"Not really," he said, looking my way. "I think cords are cool. They're retro."

Amanda pouted.

Elliot called out to me. "How's *le bras*—the arm?"

I pointed at my sling. "Sore."

Amanda grabbed him roughly and started to pull him away.

"So's mine," he said, pointing at Amanda's tight grip.

Caroline and I giggled.

Amanda looked confused. "Do you *know* her or something?" Elliot shook his head. "Nope." And then he winked at me again. Like we had our own little secret.

ELLIOT'S VOICE WAS in my head all the way home from school. *I think cords are cool. They're retro.* He said that. About me. Well, about my cords. But it was my decision to wear the cords, so that makes not only the cords cool but me as well. That's what I figured anyway. What did Elliot see in Amanda Shea? Maybe he was attracted to girls with big boobs. If that was the case, I didn't have a snowball's chance in hell. Still, he seemed to like me. He did ask me how I was. And winked at me. Twice. That must count for something. But going out with someone like Amanda? That got me worried. He must have really bad judgment. Then again, nobody's perfect.

I pictured Elliot in my head—the green eyes, the long lashes, the mop of curly hair and the dimples. I took a mental photograph so I could call it up anytime I wanted. But as soon as I walked through the front door and heard my parents fighting, the image was erased. Just like that.

"Do you know what you've cost us, Phonse? Do you? How will we live now?"

"I just needed a few bucks, that's all," said Dad. "It wasn't a firing offense. Unlawful dismissal, that's what it is."

"What's going on?" I asked.

"It doesn't concern you," said Dad.

"Oh, it certainly does concern her," said Mom. "It will concern her when she's going to school on an empty stomach. It will concern her when she's going to school dressed in rags."

"Will someone tell me what's going on here?"

"Your father here ran out of booze, and of course he needed money to buy some because God knows he doesn't have any money of his own, so he decided to come to my work, loaded drunk, to ask me for some."

Wow. That was the first time Mom had ever said it out loud. *Loaded drunk.*

"And then," she continued, "he started turning on the charm with the girls on the front cash, telling them what a fine store it was and what did they think of his wife, wasn't she grand, and would they excuse him while he had a word with that fine wife of his. All of which would have been fine and dandy if he wasn't as drunk as a skunk, slurring every word and stumbling all over the place. *I just thought I'd pop in and see if you had a few dollars,* he says. *I've lost my wallet and we've run out of milk.*

Milk—if only that were the case. I said, *You'll not be getting any money from me to buy milk—I think you've had enough milk already today*. Then he starts bawling and roaring, saying, *Me missus doesn't love me anymore—she can't even spare me a couple of dollars for milk*."

Mom was red as a beet and looked as if she had just tasted something bitter and was trying to spit the taste away with her words.

"And then," she continued, "Edward Bartlett—Mr. bloody Bartlett's himself—came in and said, *Is there a problem*? and I said, *No, my husband here is just leaving* and then your father looks at Mr. Bartlett and says, *Who's he, the cat's father*? And then I said, *Phonse, go home out of it for the love of God. You're not making any sense.* And then after some more foolishness Mr. Bartlett said, *Perhaps you should take your husband home and perhaps it would be best if you went with him.*"

"That's not fair!" I yelled.

"That's what I said," piped in Dad. "Unlawful dismissal, that's what it is."

They started in again. I wanted to go to Nan's. I wanted to sit in her kitchen. I wanted to have a nice cup of tea and listen to her old transistor. I wanted to be anywhere but here.

I KNOCKED ON Mr. Adams's door.

"I'm here to clean," I said.

Mr. Adams did his *harrumph, tsk-tsk, tut-tut* combo. "You're not due here till tomorrow, lass."

"I know. I just, um, had some free time."

"What about that arm?" he said, pointing to my sling. "You'll be as useless as a one-legged man in an arse-kickin' competition."

I laughed. "I'll manage."

"You're a bloody-minded lass." He handed me a duster. "You can start in the front room."

It was weird being in Mr. Adams's living room. We always had tea in the kitchen. I dusted the framed pictures on the mantel. So many faces. I'd never seen any visitors come to Mr. Adams's house. So who were all these people?

Mr. Adams came in to check on me. He ran his finger along a side table that I hadn't had a chance to get to. "Dust!" he exclaimed. "You, young lady, couldn't clean a house to save your bloody life. You're cack-handed and feckless. Just leave it. You might as well just sit down out of the way."

So I sat down on the couch. Mr. Adams went to the kitchen, and a few minutes later he popped into the living room and said, "Ee, you're lazy. If you're going to just sit there like a lemon doin' nought you might as well come 'ave some tea and bickies."

I joined him in the kitchen.

"Why do you say *ee*?" I asked.

"What? Ee? What are you on about, lass?"

"*Ee by gum. Ee, you're lazy. Ee, that's a crackin' knife.*"

Mr. Adams poured the tea.

"It's an expression. An exclamation, like. From the homeland." He took a big slurp of tea. "Ee, that's good tea. Get it?"

I took a sip. "Aah, that's good tea."

Mr. Adams shook his head. "*Ee* sounds better."

"I disagree. It just sounds like some random letter rather than an exclamation." I took another sip. "W, that's good tea."

"Don't make fun of my Yorkshire dialect, you cheeky little madam!"

"So who are all the people in those photos?" I asked.

Mr. Adams looked taken aback. "Oh, well, um, they're family. All dead and buried now."

"I'm sorry."

"Nay, don't be, lass. If they were still livin' I wouldn't see 'em any road."

"How come?"

"Because we stopped talkin' long, long ago."

"Why?"

"They wanted me to stay and work on the farm."

"And you wanted to follow Elspeth to Sheffield?"

"Aye. I loved the Yorkshire dales—still do. It's the best place on earth. But sheep farmin' wasn't for me.

My parents were disappointed that I left the family business. Angry, even. They said, *If you go, don't bother comin' back*. But I went anyway."

"Did you ever go back?"

"Aye, lass, I did. A few years later. I wanted 'em to meet Elspeth. Properly, like. Really get to know her."

"Did they like her?"

Mr. Adams sighed. "I was sure she'd win 'em over. But I was wrong. They were cold to her. They thought she were too grand—*too big for her britches*, they said. But they didn't know her like I did. She were a sweet lass. So down to earth. Elspeth and me needed a new start. Her parents didn't approve of me and my parents didn't approve of her. So we came to Canada and forgot about everyone else. We made a nice life here. Just the two of us."

I thought about my family. I could leave. Make a new start. Wouldn't bother me.

"Why do you have pictures of them on your mantel then," I asked, "if they were so mean to you?"

"Because at the end of the day, they're still family. There's always a bond there, and it's a hard one to break. I often wondered if we made a mistake by leavin', if we didn't try hard enough to make things work. Maybe time would 'ave healed the wounds and her family would 'ave accepted me and mine would 'ave accepted her. Who knows? Any road, it's all in the past now."

As we sat quietly and sipped our tea, I wondered if Mr. Adams was as crazy as he made himself out to be.

"Why do you sit like that?" he asked.

"Like what?"

"All twisted, like, in your chair."

I looked down. He was right. I was sitting directly across from him but twisted slightly to the left.

"Hmm, weird," I said, straightening up.

"You sit like that every time," he said.

"I do?"

"Yes, you do. It's terrible posture, you know. Terrible."

Mr. Adams changed the subject and started talking about a book called *All Creatures Great and Small*, about a vet working on the Yorkshire Dales. He went on and on and on, but I stopped listening. The posture thing was bugging me. And then it dawned on me.

"It's because my dad always sat to my right at our kitchen table," I said.

"Eh? What are you on about, lass?"

"My posture. I guess I've always sat that way, twisted to the left, so I wouldn't have to look at him. Because if I looked at him, I counted. You know, one drink, two drinks…five, six. It was like an obsession. I drove myself crazy doing it. So I guess I turned away without even realizing it." I drank my last drop of tea and shrugged. "Guess it's just habit now. Weird."

Mr. Adams seemed to have become fascinated with picking up biscuit crumbs on the tip of his finger. He did it over and over again—picked up a crumb, put it on his plate, picked up a crumb, put it on his plate. Then he coughed and said, "You sit however you like, flower."

He poured me more tea and put six biscuits on my plate. Then he went to the cupboard and pulled a box of chocolates from the highest shelf.

"My special stash," he said, opening it up and tossing a handful on top of my biscuit pile.

"Um, thanks," I said.

He put a hand on my shoulder and squeezed it. "We all 'ave troubles, don't we, love?" he said. "No one is immune."

I popped a chocolate in my mouth and nodded. He patted my shoulder once, twice, three times before telling me I was going to get as fat as a hippopotamus if I didn't stop eating all his chocolates.

PELLEY'S PHARMACY WAS big and old-fashioned and reminded me of the kind of a store you'd find in Parsons Bay, only with better stuff. There was a small cooler section with essentials like bread, milk and butter; a confection area with loads of chocolate bars, chips and ice cream; a pharmacy section with medicine, shampoos and toiletries; and a giftware department with ornaments, knickknacks, jewelry and greeting cards. Every time I went out walking to let the fresh air blow the stink of cigarette smoke off my clothes, I'd stop in. Not that I had any money to spend there, but Pelley's was a great place to browse.

The jewelry counter was my favorite.

"Whatcha getting?" said a voice behind me as I stared into the glass case.

I hadn't talked to him in weeks, not since that second day of school, but it only took me half a second to recognize Elliot's voice. I could practically feel his breath on the back of my neck. I didn't turn around.

"Nothing," I said. "Just browsing."

But I knew exactly what I was looking for. My eyes scanned the display, looking for the special item I'd admired on every one of my visits to Pelley's.

"See anything you like?" he asked.

"Well, there's a bracelet I've kinda had my eye on."

Elliot moved in even closer. "Which one is it?" he asked.

I could have described it in detail, because I had it memorized: the way the clasp worked, its seven gems all in a row, the colors of the gems and what order they were set in. Mr. Pelley, who didn't seem to mind that I spent more time than money in his store, once asked if I wanted to try it on. I said no. What was the point? It was $49.99. The money I'd earned from what little Mr. Adams paid me was for Christmas presents, not gifts for myself. And there was no point asking my parents. With Mom losing her job, $49.99 might as well have been a million dollars.

"Well?" said Elliot. "Are you going to point it out or what?"

"I'm looking," I said. "Hold on. It must be on the other side."

The jewelry sat in rows on a device kind of like a Ferris wheel inside the glass case. When you pressed a little black button on top of the counter, the rows spun in a circle. I pushed the button, letting the jewelry that didn't interest me spin by, passing the cheap rings that turned your fingers green and the earrings that turned your ears red.

"It's coming up," I said as the wheel rotated.

I had it timed perfectly. I lifted my finger off the old, worn button at just the right moment and it stopped in front of us—the treasure, my bracelet, *Genuine Sterling Silver* written on a paper tag tied to the clasp.

"That's it."

"Nice," he said. "Which stone's your favorite?"

"The purple. It's an amethyst."

"I'm impressed," he said. "What are the other stones?"

"That's the only one I know," I admitted. "And that's just because back in Parsons Bay, Betty Mahoney had an amethyst necklace and at Nan's seventieth birthday she came up to me, a drink in one hand and a cigarette in the other, saying, *Kit, my duck, come here, I shows ya something.*" I mimicked Mrs. Mahoney, pretending to be drunk and pulling an imaginary necklace away from my neck and pushing it into Elliot's face. "*Amethyst,*" I continued. *"Comes from the Greek word meaning 'sober.' You can't get drunk when you're wearing this, no matter how much you drink.*"

Elliot laughed at my impersonation.

"And what did you say?" he asked.

"I said, *Well, Mrs. Mahoney, if you ask me, your neck-lace is broken.*"

"That's hysterical."

"Yeah," I said. "She was quite the character."

Elliot pointed to the bracelet. "Are you going to get it?"

I suddenly felt embarrassed. I didn't want to say I couldn't afford it.

"I'm still thinking about," I lied.

"Cool. I'm going to get a bag of chips or something. Want anything? My treat."

"Yeah, okay. I'll have a tin of drink."

"A what?"

"A tin of drink. You know, like a can of Pepsi?"

Elliot laughed. "Never heard it called that before."

"Oh, that's just what we say at home," I said, flustered. "It's pretty dumb, actually."

"I think it's cute."

"Really?"

Elliot smiled. "I'll be right back."

He bought two cans of Pepsi, and we went behind the store to drink them. He jumped up onto a closed Dumpster and sat down.

"Come on," he said. "Climb up here and sit your bum down. Take a load off."

I raised my sling. "How am I supposed to get up there? And besides, it's dirty and it's gross."

Elliot laughed. "Don't be such a girl!"

"I have one arm, Moptop. I can't climb."

He jumped down and clasped his hands together. "Put your foot in here and I'll give you a boost. When you get up there, lean on your good arm and I'll push your arse up and over."

"You're not going anywhere near my arse."

Elliot made his voice go deadly serious. He looked me in the eye. "Our tins of drink are up there, Ms. Ryan. We have no choice but to continue with this mission."

"If I fracture my other arm…"

"You won't." He put his clasped hands down by my leg. "Hop on."

He boosted me up, and once my good elbow was on the top of the Dumpster, he pushed me the rest of the way. Before I knew it he was at the top himself, with an arm around my waist and pulling me to sitting.

"Success!" he beamed.

"For you," I said. "Seeing as you got to touch my arse."

He laughed and opened my Pepsi. "Cheers." We clinked the cans together.

"How did you know my last name was Ryan?"

He blushed. "Oh, I, um…I…you see…"

I raised my eyebrows. "I'm waiting."

He cringed. "I looked it up on your class list."

"How did you get my class list? You don't even go to my school."

He shifted uncomfortably. "There was a copy in Amanda's binder. I knew she'd have one because she worked at registration."

Ugh. Amanda.

"I don't know what you see in her," I blurted out.

"It's complicated," he said. "We're kind of the *it* couple. There's pressure."

"Pressure," I said. "Give me a break. No one has a gun to your head. And if you're so into her, why are you sitting on a Dumpster drinking Pepsi with me?"

He looked at me directly. "There's something about you, Kit."

My heart was beating like mad. I knew where he was going, and part of me really wanted him to go there. But not with Amanda in the picture.

He put his hand on my leg. "I'd really like to get to know you better. Maybe we could go out sometime."

I picked up his hand and moved it back to his own leg. "Not while you have girlfriend."

"I mean as a friend. I'm allowed to have friends, you know."

"Really? Amanda actually *allows* it? Wow, you lucky boy."

"You really don't like her, do you?"

"She's mean."

"It's all show. She's really quite sensitive deep down."

"If you say so."

"So, what do you say? Do you want to get together sometime?"

I drank the last of my Pepsi. "I gotta go."

"You didn't answer my question."

"Help me down."

Elliot hopped off the Dumpster, then reached up and eased me down, his hands around my waist. He didn't let go when my feet had safely reached the ground. The rubber tips of our sneakers were kissing.

"Well?" he said. "Can I see you again?"

His face was so close to mine, I could smell his breath. It was sweet. I swallowed hard.

"I think that would be a really bad idea."

"Why?"

"I have to go."

He took a step backward, giving me room to leave, but when I started to walk away he grabbed my arm. "Kit, wait, what if I—"

I pulled away. "Bye, Moptop."

Not until I'd turned the corner did I let my shoulders slump and my head hang. Then I dragged myself home, wishing Amanda Shea never existed.

I'D MADE THE right decision, to nip things in the bud with Elliot. Amanda was making my life a living hell; the last thing she needed was more ammunition. Caroline usually had my back, but she wasn't there every hour of every day. She wasn't there when Amanda and her friends blocked me from leaving the bathroom to tell me I was a loser who should either move back to *Joe Blow's Hole* or kill myself. She wasn't there when a single word, written in sky-blue ink, appeared on my locker: *baygirl.*

The cold October weather was my excuse to avoid the courtyard at lunchtime. Caroline and I would have a quick bite in the cafeteria before she headed off to floor hockey. Then, not wanting to look like a loser sitting alone, I'd hide in the small cloakroom at the back of my homeroom for the rest of lunch. I sat there, surrounded by expensive Nikes and Keds, in a pair of Mom's old boots. I'd outgrown my own and didn't feel like asking for new ones.

Nights were spent in my den, either writing letters to Anne-Marie that never got answered or making my way through the mountain of Sweet Valley High books that Iggy had picked up at a garage sale. The highlight of my week was cleaning day at Mr. Adams.

Iggy was getting worried. Our Wednesday nights out were full of questions. *How's school? Do you have any friends? What about this Caroline? Why don't you invite her over? Is there anything you'd like to talk about?* But I'd just say everything was fine. Iggy had enough problems.

He wouldn't give up though. He didn't know why I was unhappy, but he did everything in his power to cheer me up. When he saw that my winter coat was an ugly old army-green parka, he took me out to choose a new one. When he saw me trying, and failing, to put a decent school lunch together from the meager offerings in the fridge, he stocked up on healthy food. He even started getting up early to make my lunch—a thermos of soup or a sandwich with all the fixings. The best thing of all, though, was when he passed me the phone one evening. "Call your Nan," he said. "Don't worry about the charges. Talk as long as you like."

We were on the phone for two and a half hours. I lied and said St. John's was great. Then I changed the subject and asked about Parsons Bay. Nan told me she'd just finished harvesting all her vegetables and was putting the garden to bed. She said she'd hired a couple of young boys to help, seeing as how they had lost their part-time jobs when the fish plant shut down. She said it was quiet in Parsons Bay. She'd missed the putt-putt of the boats all summer, and the empty wharves made her sad. Then she told me the weirdest news of all. Ms. Bartlett had gotten married…to Fisty Hinks. Well, she didn't say Fisty—she used his real name, Frank. I could hardly believe it. Nan didn't know the details. She just said they were in love. I couldn't picture it, but if Ms. Bartlett was happy, I was happy too.

Before we hung up Nan gave me her Christmas pudding recipe. "Your father's favorite," she said. "Practice now so you'll have it down by December. It'll mean the world to him."

I told Nan I loved her and said goodbye. Then I crumpled up the recipe and threw it in the garbage.

WHEN MR. BYRNE announced that our class would be having a public-speaking contest, the whole class was buzzing with topic ideas. Caroline suggested Amanda write a speech called "My Life as the School Bitch" and Amanda suggested Caroline write one called "My Life as a Grungy Loser Tomboy." I had loads of topics to choose from too; I just didn't share them with the class. The titles included:

- "Shopping at Bartlett's—My Personal Agony"
- "My Father, The Idiot"
- "Living in A Dead Person's Room"
- "How Foreign Overfishing Ruined My Life"

and, simply,

- "Why My Life Sucks."

It was hard to choose. But that night, a topic came quickly. Because for the first time in my life, my father hit my mother. Mom and I were watching *Dirty Dancing* when Dad came home early from the pub.

"They cut me off," he said, falling into his recliner. "Said I'd had enough. The bastards."

I pretended he was invisible and turned up the volume.

"What's this crap?" he asked.

"A movie," I said, my eyes glued to the screen.

"*What* movie?"

Mom answered because she knew I wouldn't. "*Dirty Dancing.*"

"*Dirty Dancing*?" said my father. "Sounds like a load of filthy porn."

Mom and I couldn't help it—we looked at each other and smirked.

"What's so funny?" asked Dad.

"Nothing," I muttered.

"We were just laughing at the movie, Phonse," said Mom.

He wasn't buying it. "You were laughing at me, weren't you?"

"Don't be so paranoid," I said.

We turned our attention back to the movie, but I could feel him staring at us, full of suspicion.

Then he leapt out of his chair and snatched the remote.

"Couple of bitches," he yelled.

I felt sick to my stomach.

"You watch whatever you like," Mom said, her voice shaky.

My father settled into his chair. "I certainly will," he said. "I don't need your friggin' permission."

He put on wrestling. Mom and I didn't budge. Half an hour later he passed out in his chair. "Mom, he's asleep," I whispered. "Put the movie back on."

She looked hesitant. "I don't know, Kit."

"This is our house too," I said. "Go on. He's totally out of it."

But as soon she got up to get the remote, his eyes popped open and he lunged at her. "What are you doing, you stupid woman?"

I screamed for Iggy, but it was too late. My father had struck my mother hard across the face, sending her backward into the couch. Iggy rushed down the stairs, grabbed my father by the shoulders and pushed him against the wall. He put his hand around my dad's throat.

My mother, through her tears and her pain, begged Iggy to let my father go. "He didn't mean it, Iggy," she said. "It was my fault. I should have asked first."

"Call the police, Kit!" said Iggy.

"Don't you dare, Kitty," said my father through gritted teeth.

I reached for the phone with a shaking hand, but my mother grabbed it first.

"No one is calling the police!" she said. "He made a mistake. He's sorry. You're sorry, right, Phonse?"

He didn't answer.

I stared at my mother. "You're pathetic."

She looked wounded, cut by the honesty of my words. She lowered her head.

Iggy let go of my dad and gave him a shove. "I want you out of my house."

"If he goes, I go," said Mom.

Iggy shook his head. "Then so be it."

Mom looked at me, embarrassed but defiant. "And if I go, she goes."

"No she doesn't!" I yelled. "I'm not going anywhere!"

I ran to my room. Iggy followed.

"I can stay, right?" I said. "If you kick them out, I can stay?"

He sat down on my bed. "Of course."

"Will you kick them out? For real?"

He sighed. "I don't know, Kit. I want him out, but I don't want your mother to go with him."

"If she's stupid enough to go, let her. Who cares?"

"I care. And so do you. At least if they're here, I can keep an eye on things. She's my sister. I have to protect her."

My head was spinning. "Why did he hit her? He's never hit her before. All these years...why now?"

"Who knows?" said Iggy. "Stress? Depression? He's lost his livelihood. He's living with his brother-in-law. He's not the king of his castle anymore, Kit. He's a sad, depressed drunk."

"So what do we do?" I said. "Just live with it?"

"For now. I don't know what else to do."

"Me neither."

"I'm sorry, Kit."

"You have nothing to be sorry for."

Iggy kissed the top of my head. "It's late. Go to bed. Try to get some sleep."

But I didn't go to bed. I went downstairs to the den instead and, holding nothing back, wrote an in-your-face kind of a speech. And even though my stupid sling made it difficult, I made a poster to go with it—a visual aid, big and bold, to help drive the point home. Soon everyone would know just what a waste of space my father really was.

A BLUSH OF purple pushed through the foundation that Mom had slathered on her cheek. "What will you say if someone mentions it?" I asked. But she didn't want to talk about it. She mumbled something about a door and that was that. She didn't speak to Dad for days. Iggy had it out with him though. Big time. Laid on a major guilt trip. Dad even apologized. But the next night he was right back in his recliner, a glass in his hand and a bottle by his side.

Mr. Adams was the only person I told. He didn't say much. He just listened. And when I was done, he reached into his pocket. "How about a quarter?" he said, as if I was a five-year-old who'd be cheered up by a bit of loose change. I took it from his hand and went home, feeling better, oddly enough.

A FEW DAYS later, Iggy was waiting for me on the front step when I got home from school. He told me he'd found the poster I made. My heart sank.

"I wasn't snooping," he said. "I was just looking for some tax stuff in the den and saw it on the desk."

"That's okay," I said. "It's not like it's a secret or anything. It is a *public*-speaking contest, after all."

"So you won't mind reading me the speech that goes with it?" he asked.

"Not at all," I said, shrugging as if it was no big deal. "Whatever."

"Great. Can't wait to hear it." He opened the front door and gestured for me to go through. "After you."

I didn't move. "What? Right now?"

He nodded. "Yep. Right now."

I walked through the house as if the den were death row and Iggy a prison guard marching me to the electric chair. Iggy wouldn't like my speech. No one in my family would. But I didn't write it for them. I wrote it for me.

I sat at the desk and shuffled through the stack of loose-leaf paper, pretending to look for the speech. After a few awkward moments I realized there was no point dragging it out. I could tell by the way Iggy was looking at me that he'd waited long enough. I opened up the desk drawer and pulled out the speech.

Iggy picked up the poster. "Here," he said. "I'll be your easel."

"Thanks."

He held up the bright-yellow bristol board showing the giant liquor bottle I had drawn. I felt myself blush.

"Go ahead," he said. "Read the speech."

I fumbled with the paper, and when I scanned the first page I started to think that maybe my speech wasn't such a good idea.

"Go ahead," he said again. "Read it."

I cleared my throat.

"*Mr. Byrne, fellow students and Iggy. The topic of my speech today is…*"

I looked up. Iggy raised his eyebrows. "Go on," he said.

"*Um, the title of my speech today is, uh, 'Living with a Drunk: My Personal Experience.'*"

I looked up again to see Iggy's reaction, but he just looked back at me, straight-faced.

"*This is the Drunk-O-Meter.*" I pointed awkwardly at the bristol board. "*As you can see, I have divided this bottle into five sections, each one representing one of my alcoholic father's states of drunkenness. I have ordered them from not so bad, seen here at the bottom, to really, really bad, seen up here at the very top. I'd like to start with the bottom fifth of the bottle, The Happy Drunk. When my father is in the Happy Drunk stage, he can be found at the local pub using a piece of battered cod as a microphone and singing 'Phonse was every inch a sailor.'*"

I paused. Iggy's poker face revealed nothing.

"*Alternately,*" I continued, "*he can be found at home standing on a chair giving a speech, because, when in the Happy Drunk state of drunkenness, my father sees our family life as one of sunshine and roses. He can talk for hours about how he has the greatest family in the world and how I am the most wonderful girl in the universe. I wish I could believe him. But when I look in his bloodshot eyes it's plain to see. It's the booze talking, not his heart."*

Out of the corner of my eye, I glimpsed sadness on Iggy's face, a chink in his armor.

"Keep going," he said quietly.

"*Next up, The Legless Drunk. This state is characterized by the inability to stand up without stumbling, coupled with the inability to string a sentence together. Picture this: my father staggers through the door after a night at the pub. He falls into his chair and says—*"

I paused again. "This is dumb. I don't know why I even wrote it."

"Keep going," said Iggy. "He falls into his chair and says…"

I let out a deep sigh. "*He falls into his chair and says, 'Itty-Bitty-Kitty, my marverloush daughter, pash me a shigarette, I need a shigarette, gashping for a shigarette, need a shmoke, wheresh yer mudder, wheresh my shigarette, wheresh my shupper?'*"

I looked up. "See? It's dumb."

Iggy pointed at the speech. "Keep going."

"*But there's one positive of aspect of The Legless Drunk,*" I continued. "*It always ends with the inevitable Pass-Out.*

So before I know it, my annoying lush of a father is out cold and I can relax, for a little while at least, knowing that he can cause no trouble."

I pointed to the middle section of the liquor bottle. *"Now for The Depressed Drunk. We won't spend a lot of time here. There's not much to say, really."*

I scanned the next few lines I had written, and when I spoke, my voice started to shake a bit and I was startled by stinging in my eyes.

"Hearing my father say things like, 'What's the use? What's the bloody use? I might as well shoot myself in the head' upsets me more than anything else. Not because I'm afraid that he'll do it, but because sometimes I wish that he would."

A tear rolled down my cheek.

"It's okay, Kit, keep going," Iggy whispered, so I did, even though the page was shaking and the words were all blurry.

"Next up, The Moody Drunk. The fear of the unknown. At any moment, The Moody Drunk can snap. The Moody Drunk is unpredictable. The Moody Drunk is unreasonable. The Moody Drunk makes me wish that a magic fairy would come and sweep up the eggshells I always seem to be walking on and take them away forever."

Iggy gave me a sympathetic smile and spoke softly. "You're almost done, Kit."

I swallowed hard.

"*Last but not least, The Mad Drunk. Broken dishes and broken hearts. Blushes on faces and bruises on cheeks. Fists that shake and eyes that threaten. Words that swirl in the air like gusts of snow riding on the breeze, never to be caught.*"

I took a tissue from the box on the desk and wiped my eyes. "That's it," I said. "I didn't really know how to wrap it up."

Iggy put the poster down.

"You know you can't read that at school, right, Kit?"

I nodded.

"I mean, social services would be all over this place."

"It seemed like a good idea at the time," I said. "But now that I've read it…I mean, I could never have read that in front of my whole class. I don't know what I was thinking."

Iggy took me by the arm and sat me on the couch. "You were mad. At your dad. So you wrote about him. And very well, too, I might add."

I blew my nose. "Really?"

"Yep. Really. And I bet it felt good to get it all on paper too, huh?"

"Yeah, it did, actually. It felt really good."

"You should write more often then," he said. "I'll get you a journal, if you like."

"You will?"

"Sure."

Iggy got up and took my speech off the desk. "What should we do with this? We wouldn't want it to fall into the wrong hands."

"Rip it up," I said.

He passed it to me. "No. You rip it up."

So I did. Into a million little pieces.

I WAS IN Mr. Adams's kitchen, leaning against the mop handle and staring into the bucket of murky water, when he burst in and accused me of being the worst house-cleaner in the history of the world.

"Sorry," I said. "I was thinking."

"I don't pay you to think, lass. I pay you to keep things spick-and-span."

I took the mop out of the bucket and slopped it onto the floor.

"Sorry," I said again. "I have a lot on my mind."

Mr. Adams grabbed the mop out of my hand. "Obviously," he grumbled. "Look at the ginormous puddle you just threw on the floor. It looks like the bloody Atlantic ocean in here."

I held up my sling. "Mopping's a bit awkward."

"Excuses, excuses." He wrung out the mop, dipped it in the puddle and let it soak up the water, then wrung it out again.

"Bloody hell, this is hard work," he said, wiping his brow. "Why didn't you tell me it was this hard?"

"Well, I—"

"Come on," he said. "Break time. 'Ave a seat. I'll make the tea."

I sat at the kitchen table and, while Mr. Adams filled the teapot with hot water, put my head down on my arms, closed my eyes and tried to think of a new topic for my speech.

"Wake up, lass!" Mr. Adams boomed. "Don't you know it's the height of rudeness to fall asleep at the table?"

"I'm thinking," I said, sitting up straight.

"So you keep saying," he said. He placed two cups and the teapot on the table.

"Any bickies?" I asked.

"Listen here, madam," Mr. Adams huffed. "You shouldn't ask for bickies. You should wait to be offered. Coming out and asking like that is the height of rudeness. The height of rudeness, I say!"

"What *isn't* the height of rudeness?" I grumbled.

"Kit Whatever-your-name is! You are in a foul mood today!"

"It's Ryan. And like I said, I have a lot on my mind."

Mr. Adams got up, grabbed some biscuits out of the cupboard and presented them to me.

"Will these do, Your Royal Pain in the Arse?" he asked.

"Yes." I laughed. "They'll do. And I'm sorry. You're right. I have been the height of rudeness. The width of rudeness too."

Mr. Adams poured tea into my cup. "A problem shared is a problem halved, you know."

I sighed. "I have to write a speech. For school. I mean, I already wrote one. About my dad. But it was a bit too honest, if you know what I mean, and now I have to start all over again, and I can't think of a new topic."

Mr. Adams thought for a moment. "Then don't change it."

"Huh? What do you mean?"

He shrugged. "Don't change the topic. Try to turn a negative into a positive. Write about your dad again but in a good way, and see what happens."

I looked at him like he was nuts. "If I write a speech about my dad and try to make it positive, it'll be a speech full of big fat lies, because there is nothing, and I mean nothing, positive about that man."

"There's good in everybody, flower," he said, waving his biscuit in the air. "You just 'ave to look a wee bit closer with some folk."

"A wee bit closer?" I snorted. "I'd need X-ray vision to find good in my dad."

Mr. Adams chuckled. "It'll be a challenge, that's for sure. But give it some thought, lass. You never know what you might come up with."

I finished my tea and went home. All through supper and all through homework, I racked my brain, only to come up empty. Lying in bed, I searched every file in my head for something positive about my dad. The only result was a pounding headache.

But when I woke up in the morning, a memory came to me right out of the blue, like a big whack across the face.

I went to school and spent my lunch hour in the cloakroom, writing. The words flowed out like a glass of spilled milk, flooding every inch of the page, soaking into every corner, and when the last drops had dribbled out, I mopped up the messy bits, tidying here and there, until I was left with a clean piece of writing I was proud of.

I had done it. I had found good in my father.

And I didn't even need X-ray vision.

IT WAS AGONY having a last name beginning with *R* when teachers insisted on doing things in alphabetical order. By the time Allison Johnston was reading her speech, "The Life and Times of Madonna," I was ready to jump out of my seat. And when Mr. Byrne finally called my name, that's exactly what I did. I jumped to my feet and practically ran to the podium.

I was surprised at how quickly my speech went. I mean, one minute I was standing in front of the class, reading, and the next I was back at my desk, with my heartbeat slowing to its regular pace.

I was also surprised when I won. Mr. Byrne said he really liked my "artistic approach to an informative speech." I was pretty pleased with myself, but then he went and ruined it by telling me I would have to read it again at a public-speaking night, where I would be competing with all the winners from other classes.

"Don't forget to tell your parents, Kit," he said. "Friday night, seven PM, in the auditorium."

I didn't want to tell Mom and Dad. First of all, Dad would probably show up drunk, second of all, Mom would probably be hurt that my speech wasn't about her, and, third of all, I didn't really want Dad to hear me say niceish things about him.

But I knew they'd get wind of it sooner or later, so I told them about it casually, trying to pass it off as no big deal.

"There's a public-speaking thingie at school on Friday night," I said. "Parents are invited, but it's not like you have to go or anything."

"What kind of thingie?" asked Mom.

"A contest or something."

"Are you in it?" she asked.

"Yeah, I kinda won a speech contest for my class."

"Marvelous!" she exclaimed.

"What's the topic?" asked Dad.

"It's sorta about Parsons Bay…and stuff."

"Sounds wonderful," said Mom. "We'll be there, won't we, Phonse?"

"You betcha!" said Dad.

Iggy knew what I'd been trying to do but didn't know why.

"Don't you want us to come?" he asked me later, when Mom and Dad were out of earshot.

"Um, yeah. Of course," I said. "It's kinda complicated, that's all."

"I won't let him show up drunk," he said, "if that's what you're worried about."

"That's the least of my worries," I said.

Iggy looked confused. "What do you mean?"

"I don't want him to hear the speech," I said.

"Who? Your dad?"

I nodded. "Yeah. 'Cause it's about him. And it's positive."

Iggy looked surprised. "Oh. Well, that's…nice," he said.

"Yeah, but he might think it means we're all buddy-buddy or something."

"Then why did you write it?"

"It was Mr. Adams's idea," I said. "Not mine."

"But *you* wrote it," said Iggy.

"Yeah, but—"

"And it won. So it must be pretty good."

"Yeah, but—"

"If you have something positive to say about your dad, why don't you want to share it with him?"

"I dunno. I just don't want him to be all *Look at me, I'm such a great father my daughter even wrote a speech about me.*"

"I see where you're coming from, Kit. I really do. But if you wrote something nice about your dad, why not show him? He's an idiot, I know. And he hasn't been the best father. But he's a human being, Kit. And human beings don't live forever. I don't want you to have any regrets. Let him hear your speech. Throw the man a bone."

I shrugged. "Maybe you're right."

"And besides, you've asked him now. What are you going to do? Un-invite him?"

"No, that would be the height of rudeness."

Iggy laughed. "The height of rudeness?"

"It's a Mr. Adams-ism," I said.

"Are you going to ask him along as well?"

"Who? Mr. Adams? To public-speaking night?"

"Sure. Why not?" said Iggy.

I thought for a moment. "Yeah, okay. The more the merrier."

Iggy grinned. "That's the spirit."

I ran next door and invited Mr. Adams. He told me that he'd look at his social calendar and, barring any previous engagements, consider showing up if there was nothing good on the telly.

MOM DIDN'T GET to dress up much, so on the night of the public-speaking contest she made her hair all big, put in a pair of giant hoop earrings and wore a patterned, neon wrap dress that I hadn't seen her wear since I was eight. It looked like she was going to a disco. Dad, on the other hand, wore the suit he got married in—overkill, if you ask me, but it was either that or his old work pants and plaid shirt; he had nothing in between. His accessories were his telltale bloodshot eyes and bright red nose. Iggy looked normal and respectable. I hoped he would be mistaken for my father. At the last minute, while we were all piling into Dad's old Buick, Mr. Adams came out of his house, said the telly was on the blink and hopped into the car.

We sat through a wide range of speeches. One girl wrote about the movie *Buffy the Vampire Slayer*, another about being a competitive gymnast and another about life as a twin. Then I heard my name being called.

I made my way to the podium. I heard Dad call out, "Way to go!" There was some chuckling. What was he doing? I hadn't even done anything yet.

I cursed the sling as I fumbled with the microphone, trying to get it adjusted to my height. Apparently, a midget had spoken before me.

Then I began.

Judges, teachers and fellow students: The speech I have written is entitled "This Place Where I Live: A Childhood Memory of Parsons Bay."

I cleared my throat and tried to battle my nerves.

Red, orange, yellow, green, blue, indigo, violet. Every color of the rainbow. That's what the houses are like where I live. A ruby-red house with yellow trim and a bright-blue door. A robin's-egg-blue house with green trim and a butter-yellow door.

Windy, rainy, cold, sunny, snowy. That's what the weather's like where I live. Sometimes all in one day.

It's a regular old day in Parsons Bay. And on regular old days I go to the top of the cliff. The trail twists and turns and I'm winded by the time I reach my favorite spot. I sit on a boulder and look out over the Atlantic. It's not raining, but my cheeks are wet. The air smells of salt. I can hardly see my hand in front of my face. A real pea-souper, Nan would say.

I can't see the ocean, but I can smell it. I can't see the seagulls, but I can hear them. I can't see the ships yet either, but I know they are there.

I sit for ages. I am shivering, chilled to the bone, but still I stay, in my favorite spot at the top of the cliff.

Then, I see it…just barely…the boat. Back from a day of fishing. I'm too far away to read what's painted on the side, but its letters are blue, the same sky blue that streaks my Dad's coveralls. Then I know it's the Kitty Charmer. The best vessel on the Atlantic. The one named for me.

I usually just watch from a distance. But on this regular old day in Parsons Bay, I decide to have a race. I run down the trail as fast I can, keeping an eye on the boat as it enters the bay. I go so fast I slip and slide down the steep bit, stones flying in my wake. When I get to the bottom I jump over the boulders that mark the head of the trail and beat it to the dock. I've won. I sit on the beach rocks, catching my breath, and watch as the Kitty Charmer sails in, smooth as silk.

I wait for my father. It takes ages. There's unloading and weighing and selling to be done. But, still, I wait.

He looks surprised to see me.

"Hungry?" he asks as we walk down the dock.

I nod.

"Me too," he says. "And thirsty. Wanna come to the pub?"

Mom would be mad, but I nod again.

I wonder if kids are allowed in the pub.

We head back to town.

A man and his dog walk by. "I'm tellin' ya, b'y. It's some cold out today," he says to us.

"It is indeed," says Dad.

"And the fog," continues the man. "Thick as pea soup. Never saw the likes of it."

The old man pulls up the collar of his coat and continues on. I try to wiggle my toes in my boots. They've gone numb.

An old woman walks by.

"Will you just look at her," she says, looking at me. "She's froze to death, the poor thing." And then to my dad, "You better get that child inside, my duckie. She'll catch her death out here."

My dad just laughs and rolls his eyes and we keep walking. I look ahead. The brightly colored houses stand out in the fog. They remind me of the fluorescent-orange buoys I saw bobbing in the ocean moments ago. The salt air is mixed with food smells now, half salty/ half sweet. We're near the pub.

Dad opens the door. The fiddle, the accordion and a blast of heat bombard us. People sing from their tables. Some of them raise their glasses to us and smile. "Oh, God love her, look at her red cheeks," someone exclaims.

Funny, warm, friendly, inviting. That's what the people are like where I live. "The salt of the earth," says Dad, as we are welcomed into the pub.

He introduces me to everyone as "his Kitty Charmer" and his voice is proud. I beam in his shadow.

He has a giant glass of a dark drink. But I won't tell Mom. He buys me a plate of chips. He sings along to the music. He laughs and jokes with the crowd. He's the life of the party. And he's my dad.

He dances all the way home. "Dance with me, Kitty, dance with me." So between fits of laughter we skip and jig and step-dance through the streets of Parsons Bay.

"What a marvelous place to be," he says, arms in the air, spinning in circles in the middle of an old dirt road as if he wants to grab his surroundings and hold them near.

I look around and I agree. I love it here, this place where I live.

Thank you.

The auditorium filled with applause. I scanned the audience until I saw him. We locked eyes. His were shiny. My instinct was to look away, but I didn't. For a second I thought he might, but he didn't either. Instead he winked and stuck up two thumbs.

I didn't win, but the way Mom carried on in the lobby, anyone would have thought I did. She said my speech was wonderful and amazing and brilliant, even the parts about the pub. She called Mr. Byrne over to where we were standing and said, "Wasn't she marvelous?" and he said, "Yes, she certainly was," and I was embarrassed but happy at the same time. Iggy was beaming. When Mr. Byrne said he ran a writing group and would I like to join, Iggy answered for me, saying, "Yes, she definitely would!" and I didn't mind a bit because that would have been my answer anyway.

Even Mr. Adams seemed impressed. "You're no Emily Brontë—who was from Yorkshire, by the way," he said, "but you weren't too shabby, not too shabby at all."

And while all this was going on, Dad stood in the background until Iggy took a step back and said, "Come on over, Phonse."

Dad took a step forward. He stood next to me, shifting from foot to foot, then patted me on the head like I was a toddler who had just done something really clever. "Good job, Kitty," he said. "Good job."

When we got home, Dad said we should celebrate. But we all knew what that meant. So we sat around and discussed the other speeches just long enough for Dad to have one drink. Then we all went our separate ways and left Dad alone in his chair to gnaw on the bone I had thrown him, savoring every last morsel, until nothing was left but tiny sharp fragments.

FIVE
Digestive Biscuits And World Chaos

Finally, after six long weeks, my sling was removed. The doctor said the bone had healed wonderfully and I could resume normal activities. So after a celebratory ice cream with Uncle Iggy, I went to Mr. Adams's house to give his skirting boards a good two-handed scrub. But first, we got to talking about Mr. Byrne's writing group.

"I'm pleased for you, lass," said Mr. Adams. "Chuffed to bits. You must be 'appy as a pig in muck."

I was surprised by his enthusiasm. "Well, yeah. But I wouldn't go that far. I mean, it's just a writing group."

"Just a writin' group?" he yelled. "It's more than that, lass. It's therapy! Writin' is good for what ails you. I write letters meself. Just wrote one this week, as it 'appens."

"Really? To who?"

"To whom," he said. "You'd think you'd know the proper English language by now."

"Ee by gum!" I declared. "Now that's the pot calling the kettle black."

Mr. Adams laughed. "You're a right gobby little mare, you know that, lass?"

I ignored him. "To whom?"

"To perfect strangers."

"Strangers?"

"Do you need your ears checked? Yes, strangers. This week, for example, I 'ave written to the president of Campbell's soup."

"Why?"

"Because last week I opened a can of chicken noodle and the bloody noodles were all different lengths. Can you imagine? If you ask me, they should be uniform length. *Mmm, mmm good,* my arse!"

I was afraid to ask my next question, but I found myself strangely interested.

"Who else do you write to?"

"Prison inmates."

"Oh, I've heard of that kind of thing—writing letters of support so they are not so lonely."

"Aye, *some* people write those kinds of letters. I start my letters off with 'thinking of you' rubbish in case some prison authority decides to read it, but further down in the letter I convey a very different message."

I was even more afraid to ask the next question.

"What kind of message?"

"I just like to remind 'em of why they're there, like…that they brought it on themselves by being the moral decay of society, the scum of the earth, the lowest of the low. I like to tell 'em that the world is a safer place because they're locked up and I hope that they never get to see the light of day. And then I tell 'em that they deserve worse than what they got—after all, they're living in the lap of bloody luxury with their TVs and their videos and their gyms and their three meals a day. They live better than most poor people in Third World countries. It's disgustin'. So while they are sittin' there living the high life, I like to remind 'em with a little letter that they are rotten, rotten people."

I didn't know what to say.

"Now," said Mr. Adams cheerfully, "how 'bout some tea and bickies?"

"Don't you want me to do some housework?" I waved my slingless arm. "Look. I can do it properly today."

"What's the point? It never looks any different anyway, sling or no sling. You, my dear, don't use enough elbow grease. Might as well sit here and 'ave a cuppa."

"But I feel bad about getting paid for doing nothing," I said.

Mr. Adams nodded in agreement. "Aye," he said. "I know. It's highway bloody robbery, that's what it is. Takin' advantage of a poor old man like me. It's shockin.'"

"Well, I wouldn't go that far," I said. "But still, maybe you shouldn't pay me on the days that you say that I'm too useless, lazy, idle and cack-handed to work."

Mr. Adams burst out laughing. "Kit, flower," he said, "I'd pay you just for the entertainment value."

He put the pot of tea on the table and stretched the tea cozy over it. He took a digestive biscuit out of the package. "Misshapen," he said.

"What?"

"Misshapen. Digestive biscuits should be perfectly round. This is a bloody wonky oval. Just look at it."

"Looks okay to me."

He handed me a pen and paper. "Take this down, Kit.

Dear Mr. McVitie,

I have been a long-time consumer of your digestive biscuits. I particularly enjoy the milk chocolate ones, but of course will take the plain ones if my local corner shop hasn't had the foresight to keep the shelves fully stocked of the milk chocolate ones. I mean, really, is there any need to ever run out of stock? Wouldn't it be logical that when you see that your shelves are being depleted, you order more stock in anticipation? Bad management—that's what it comes down to.

Speaking of bad management, you must be having a spot of trouble in that department yourself, for just moments ago I picked up one of your digestive biscuits and noticed that it had a peculiar shape. It wasn't round, as it should be, but a weird misshapen oval. Where was your quality control the day that biscuit was made?

You might say, 'Oh, it's only one biscuit that slipped though the cracks,' but if one is allowed to slip through, who's to say what could happen next? If your quality-control people are getting lax, who's to say that I won't be the only victim of the wonky digestive biscuit? I say nip it in the bud! I say get control! We don't want to live in a world that is disproportionate, imbalanced, unequal, unsymmetrical. We need a world that is consistent, unvarying, orderly, reliable. Otherwise, mark my words, there will be chaos.

Sincerely,
Reginald Adams

In all of his excitement, Mr. Adams started coughing. I got him some water, and while he was drinking it, I patted his back. He started to choke.

"What the bloody hell are you doing? Are you tryin' to kill me?"

"I was just trying to help."

"Well, don't."

He picked up the letter and gave it a once-over. "Your writin' is atrocious."

"Thanks."

"Thanks? It's not a bloody compliment." He passed me a dictionary. "Look it up. Atrocious."

I flipped to the *As* and scanned the page.

Mr. Adams let out a huge huff. "*A…T…R…*"

"I know how to spell it. Geez, give me a chance." I ran my finger down the page. "Here it is. 'Exceptionally bad; abominable.'"

"Now use it in a sentence."

"The disproportionate, imbalanced, unequal, unsymmetrical, misshapen digestive biscuit is atrocious."

Mr. Adams laughed so hard his coughing fit started again.

MR. BYRNE'S WRITING group met in the library every Tuesday during lunch hour. When I walked into my first meeting, I was surprised to see that some of the students were from the boys' school and even more surprised to see that Elliot was one of them. I couldn't believe how much his face lit up when he saw me. I felt embarrassed and excited at the same time.

The group had been discussing poetry. Mr. Byrne asked if anyone had anything they'd like to read.

Elliot raised his hand.

My palms went sweaty. I felt nervous for him and wished I didn't.

His poem was amazing. It was like a song. It didn't rhyme or anything, but it had this rhythm, and everything he described, well, it was like I could smell it and taste it and feel it.

I could hardly breathe.

His words whirled in my head.

I found myself wishing, once again, that Amanda Shea didn't exist.

"Nice poem," I said when the meeting ended.

Elliot smiled. "Really?"

"Really. It was amazing."

Elliot took a stack of papers out of his backpack. "Keep me company for a few minutes? I have to put up these flyers."

I followed him into the hall. He stopped at the first bulletin board.

"Hey," he said. "You got your thingie off."

I held up my arm. "Yep."

"Good," he said, shoving the stack into my arms. "You can help."

I looked at the top flyer. "Your school is hosting a winter dance?"

Elliot held four thumbtacks between his lips while he lined up the paper evenly on the board.

"Ugh, don't do that," I said. "What if you swallow one?"

"If I didn't know better," he murmured, the tacks moving up and down in his mouth, "I'd think—"

"Stop talking!" I yelled. "You're going to friggin' choke!"

Elliot gave a stifled laugh, then removed the thumbtacks one by one and pinned the flyer, perfectly straight, to the board.

"If I didn't know better," he said again, "I'd think you really care about me."

"I just don't know the Heimlich maneuver, that's all."

"Yeah, sure," he said, picking up his backpack and moving down the hall. "So where've you been lately? I haven't seen you in the courtyard in ages."

"A group of us hang out in the cloakroom at lunchtime."

"The cloakroom?"

"Yeah. We sneak in when the teachers aren't looking. We spend the whole hour back there. It's a good laugh."

"Sounds like you're settling in pretty well."

"Yep."

Elliot ripped some old flyers off the next bulletin board and held out his hand. I passed him a flyer from the stack.

"So you gonna come to the dance?" he asked.

I shrugged. "I dunno. Maybe."

He took a step in closer to me. "I miss seeing you around."

I took a step back. "I'm gonna be late for science."

He touched the sleeve of my sweater. "Meet me after school. At Pelley's."

I pulled my arm away. "No."

"I'll buy you a tin of drink," he said with a grin.

The harder he tried to win me over, the more uninterested I acted. "No, thanks," I said, turning my back to him. "I'm hanging with friends later."

Hoping my lie sounded convincing, I stuck my nose in the air and strutted away.

"Hey, Kit!" he called.

I turned around and rolled my eyes. "The answer is still no, Moptop. Move on."

He pointed at the stack of paper in my arms. "My flyers?"

I walked back to him, trying to keep my dignity intact, and shoved the pile into his hands.

"You look gorgeous when you're embarrassed," he said, a huge smirk plastered across his face.

I bit my lip to keep from smirking too. "Goodbye, Elliot."

Sitting in science class, I wondered how long my willpower would last.

THE NEXT DAY at lunchtime, the cloakroom door swung open. It was Amanda.

I jumped up. "What are you doing here?"

"You're a whore," she said. "*Haitch-O-R-E*. Whore."

I managed a convincing laugh despite the quaver in my voice. "And you're dumb. *D-U-M-B*. Dumb. *Whore* is spelled with a *w*."

Her face turned red. "You'd know," she said.

"You don't need to be a whore to know how to spell it. You just need to be literate. You know, *literate*? Able to read and write?"

"I didn't know baygirls could do either."

"I didn't know townies were stuck-up snobs with their heads up their arses."

Amanda pushed me up against the wall. "Stay away from Elliot."

"What are you talking about?"

"My friends saw you cozying up to Elliot yesterday."

"He was the one cozying up to me."

She put her face an inch away from mine. "Do you really think he'd go for someone like you? Why don't you go back to where you came from?"

There was no way I was going to let the tears that filled my eyes spill. I put my hands on her shoulders and pushed her so hard she fell over. "Go to hell, Amanda."

Scared of what she'd do next, I bolted out of the cloak-room. I ran to my locker and grabbed my backpack. Minutes later I was at Mr. Adams's house, trembling and out of breath.

"Bloody 'ell, lass. You look like you could use a cuppa."

He didn't ask what was wrong; he just made the tea and opened some biscuits.

"Did you tell 'em you were leaving?"

I shook my head.

Mr. Adams phoned the school. He said he was Kit Ryan's grandfather and was visiting from the Yorkshire Dales, a most marvelous, magical place. Then he said, "Kit had to come home today, with no time to notify a teacher, as it was a family matter of the utmost urgency."

He hung up the phone and sat back down. "Now," he said, "*As The World Turns* starts in ten minutes. You can stay if you promise to keep your trap shut."

I HAD ABSOLUTELY no intention of going to the dance, but Caroline spent weeks wearing me down.

"Come on," she said. "My other friends wouldn't be caught dead at the dance, but there's this guy I like and I know he'll be there. Please? You never know—you might meet someone yourself."

"I don't want to meet anyone. Guys suck."

"Come on, Kit, please?"

"I dunno…"

"Please, please, please?"

"It's not my scene."

"It's not mine either, but this guy…he's amazing. He plays in a band and he's so cute and I know he'll be there because a friend of a friend knows him, so I have to be there because this friend of a friend said they'd make an introduction and—"

"Okay, okay. Geez. Yes, I'll go, if it'll shut you up about it."

She smiled. "Mission accomplished."

I used my housecleaning money and bought a denim miniskirt from the Denim Den.

Mom looked me up and down. "The skirt's a bit short."

"That's the style," I said. "All the girls at school are wearing them."

Dad snorted. "They all look like sluts, do they?"

"Phonse!" Mom said.

"That's a terrible thing to say to your daughter," Uncle Iggy said.

I grabbed my jacket and stormed out, slamming the door extra hard.

Mr. Adams, who was outside drawing a picture of a pygmy shrew on his sign, looked up and said, "Did you forget your keks?"

"My what?"

"Your trousers."

"No," I huffed. "I did not."

He stood back, admired his handiwork, then leaned forward and drew a pair of pants on the shrew. "There, that's better."

I rolled my eyes. "That's ridiculous."

"No," he said, pointing at my bare legs. "*That's* ridiculous."

"What's everyone's problem? It's just a skirt."

Mr. Adams wagged his magic marker at me. "A *skirt* that might *assert* that you're a *flirt* which might *alert* some weird *per-vert* that you're *dessert*." Then he pointed at the shrew. "His name is Bert."

"Are you serious?"

"Deadly. It's short for Bertram."

"Not about the stupid shrew," I said. "About the skirt. Are you seriously saying that it would be *my* fault if some creep bothered me because of what I wore? And what's with this *dessert* thing? I mean, who says that?"

Mr. Adams ignored me. "What do you think, Bert? Should Kit go back inside and change?" He stared at the shrew for a few seconds, nodded, then turned to me. "Bert thinks you should go home and put on a pair of trousers."

I walked up to the sign. "Bert? Mind your own business."

I hadn't noticed Caroline coming up behind me. She tapped me on the back.

"Geez, Caroline!" I said. "Give me a heart attack, why don't you! Where the hell did you come from?"

Mr. Adams tutted. "Language, Kit, language."

"Oh, I'm ever so sorry. Let me rephrase that. Eh, up, lass! Where the bloody hell did you come from?"

Caroline looked confused. "Why are you talking weird? And why were you talking to a mouse?"

"A mouse?" yelled Mr. Adams. "A bloody mouse?"

Caroline looked at me and widened her eyes as if to say, "Who's the nutcase?"

"Caroline, meet Mr. Adams," I said. "Mr. Adams, Caroline."

Mr. Adams held out his hand. "Sir Reginald Adams. Kit's neighbor. May I say that your trousers are wonderfully appropriate?"

Caroline looked even more confused. I linked my arm through hers and pulled her away. "Goodbye, Mr. Adams."

"Remember," he called after me. "Don't be someone's dessert."

I had no intention of it. The way the gym smelled, I wouldn't have gone near anyone with a ten-foot pole. It was stuffy and sweaty and suffocating. After half an hour of leaning against the wall, Caroline and I decided to go outside for air. We didn't get very far. Elliot appeared in the doorway and blocked me.

"Hello, *mon petit agneau perdu*," he said, staggering and falling against me. "How'd ya like to shlow dansh with me?"

I was stunned. Moptop was drunk.

"Get out of my way."

"C'mon," he said, looking me up and down like some kind of creepy pervert. "I know you want to."

"Leave her alone, asshole," said Caroline.

He grabbed me by the arm. I flinched.

"You're hurting me."

Caroline pulled on his shoulder. "Let go of her!"

"Lesh shlow dansh, Kit. You. And me."

Amanda stumbled out the gym doors. "What's going on?" She reeked of booze.

"Ask your boyfriend," Caroline said.

"I just wanna dansh."

Caroline grabbed Elliot and shoved him out of the way. Hard. He fell over.

"Come on, Kit," she said. "Let's go home."

"What the hell is wrong with you, Elliot?" Amanda screamed. "Why would you want to dance with that ugly baygirl?"

But she didn't get an answer. Elliot was too busy puking in a trash can.

IGGY WAS UP when I got home.

"How was the dance?" he asked.

I plunked down on a kitchen chair and dropped my head to the table.

"That bad, huh?"

"Yep."

Iggy laughed. "I'll make you a cup of cocoa."

He warmed some milk on the stove, and soon the smell of cocoa filled the room. I breathed deeply and closed my eyes. The bad feeling from the dance was fading. Someone was making me cocoa. I started to imagine I was at Nan's but realized I didn't have to. It was okay here with Iggy. I didn't need to escape.

"Are you okay, Kit?"

"Just a bit tired."

"You know, Kit," said Iggy, "anytime you want to get away from…stuff…you just need to ask. I can drive you anywhere you want to go. The movie theater, the library, the mall. Anywhere." Iggy stirred the pot. "I don't even have to stay with you if you don't want me to. I could just drop you off. I understand that you mightn't want to be seen with an old man like me."

"You're not old," I said.

Iggy turned around and smiled. "See? That's why you're my favorite niece."

I laughed. "I'm your only niece, Iggy!"

"That joke never gets old," he said, placing a bowlful of mini marshmallows on the table.

He passed me a steaming mug of cocoa. I took a big sip. It warmed me from the tip of my toes to the top of my head.

I sank back in my chair and relaxed.

"You know, Iggy," I said, "I wish you *were* old."

"What? Why?"

"Because then people might mistake you for my father."

Iggy looked at me sadly. "Oh, Kit."

I threw a couple of marshmallows in my mug. "He's so embarrassing."

"I know."

"What were you and your parents thinking, letting Mom marry an asshole like that?"

Iggy took a sip of his drink. "The more we tried to tell her he was bad news, the more she attached herself to him."

"He won't change, will he?"

"There's always hope, Kit."

"I hate him."

Iggy didn't tell me it was wrong to say such things.

"I know, Kit," he said. "I know."

And I just sat there, swirling my cocoa, watching a marshmallow get caught up in the deep, dark vortex.

THE DAY AFTER the dance, Elliot was on Iggy's doorstep.

"Are you stalking me now?" I said.

"I just want to talk."

"Well, I don't want to talk to you."

"Ten minutes. That's all I ask."

"No."

Elliot stuck his foot in the door as I tried to shut it.

"Get lost, Moptop."

He tried to turn on the charm, flashing his signature smile. I'd read once that dimples were technically a birth defect. I'd say it was more like hitting the genetic lottery. Those indents were the cutest things I'd ever seen.

He added raised eyebrows to his winning smile. "*Je suis désolé.*"

"Apology not accepted. And enough with the French. It's annoying."

"Look, I'm sorry. I was a complete jerk."

"Um, *duh*! That's pretty obvious. Tell me something I don't know."

His face turned serious. "Give me ten minutes and I'll explain."

"Ten minutes," I said. "That's it."

"Not here," he said. "Let's go to Pelley's."

"Tin of drink?" he said when we got to the store.

"No thank you." I went directly to the back of the building and leaned against the Dumpster, crossing my arms. "Well?"

Elliot looked down at his feet. "Something happened the morning of the dance. Something bad."

I let my arms drop. "Yeah?"

Elliot dug a groove in the gravel with the toe of his shoe. "My grandfather died. In his sleep. Mom asked me not to go to the dance. She asked me to stay home. But I went anyway. I said, *He's dead now. What difference does it make?* And she cried. And I felt like shit for making her cry. And I felt like shit because my grandpa was dead. So I drank Amanda's disgusting booze so I wouldn't feel like shit anymore."

I was stunned. "Wow."

He ran his fingers nervously through his hair. "So… I'm sorry, okay? I really am."

"Did it work?"

"What?"

"The booze. Did it help you not feel like shit anymore?"

He shook his head. "Nah, it made me feel worse."

"Good."

"I just want you to know how sorry I am."

"Saying sorry doesn't cut it."

I started to leave. Part of me didn't want to, but I thought about all the times my mother had forgiven my father so easily, so pathetically. I wasn't going to give in to a simple sorry. As I walked away, I heard a series of thumps. I turned around. Elliot was kicking the Dumpster in frustration.

I gave him a round of applause. "Bravo, bravo," I said. "Nice show."

He looked up, and I was startled by the mixture of surprise and sadness in his face. "Wow," he said quietly. "You don't forgive easily, do you?"

"What do you mean?" I said. "I forgive. I forgive people all the time."

Elliot leaned against the Dumpster and slid down to the ground. "In Mr. Byrne's writing group, we did this funny writing exercise where we had to think up fortune-cookie sayings. He gave us this printout of famous quotes, for inspiration. And there was this one that I really liked. It was *To forgive is to set a prisoner free and discover that the prisoner was you.*"

I rolled my eyes. "So what are you saying? I'm only hurting myself by not forgiving you?"

"Not exactly," he said. "Because I feel hurt too. But to hold all that anger in…geez, Kit. That can't be good."

I leaned against the brick wall of Pelley's. "Wow," I said. "You're a master at turning things around. This isn't about me being some kind of a prisoner with anger issues. This is about you getting drunk and acting like a moron."

"Fair enough, Kit, I was a moron. But I've apologized. What do you want, blood?"

I shrugged. "Maybe."

"When was the last time you forgave someone?"

"What?"

"You said, *I forgive people all the time.* So when was the last time you forgave someone?"

I thought of my dad, who I would never, ever forgive, as long as I lived.

I walked over and sat down next to Elliot.

"Okay, so maybe you're right. Maybe I don't forgive easily."

"I understand why you're so mad, Kit, but—"

"No, you don't. You don't understand. See, the thing is, my father is an alcoholic."

"What?"

"My father. He's a drunk."

He was stunned. "Wow."

"So maybe I have a stronger reaction to drunkenness than most people. But you disgusted me. The way my father disgusts me every single day of my life. And I'm never going to forgive him for that. So, yeah, I'm a prisoner, all right. And maybe forgiveness would set me free, but the thing is, it would also let my dad off the hook."

He put his head in his hands. "I'm sorry, Kit."

He really was sweet. Deep down I knew that. He hadn't meant to hurt me. But he was way out of line at the dance. Getting drunk like that? Grabbing my arm? Unforgivable.

I put my hand on his shoulder as I stood up. "You're a nice guy, Elliot. If you want to drink, fine. But don't expect to be friends with me. Because I have enough bullshit to deal with."

Elliot grabbed my hand. "Don't go."

I pulled away. "Goodbye, Elliot."

"Kit! Please!"

I walked away, wishing things were different.

"Kit, wait!"

He was behind me, tugging on my coat. "Stop."

I turned around. "You had your ten minutes."

"I want us to be friends."

I threw my hands up in the air. "Friends?" I said. "Being friends with you is too complicated. I don't need the hassle."

"Actually, I want to be more than friends," he said.

"What?"

"I broke up with Amanda."

My heart skipped a beat. "You did?"

"After the dance. She was no good for me, Kit. We're finished."

My prayers had been answered. Amanda Shea didn't exist anymore. I thought that would change everything. But it didn't. The Elliot standing in front of me now may have been sweet and charming and kind, but the drunken, obnoxious Elliot from the dance was still fresh in my mind.

I STARTED FINDING poems everywhere—in my locker, in my coat pocket, in Iggy's mailbox. I even found one taped to the glass display at Pelley's. Seeing them signed "Anonymous" made me laugh every time. They were love poems, and they were lovely. If only Elliot hadn't been drunk at the dance. Caroline didn't understand why I wouldn't forgive him. I couldn't tell her that I'd feel like a hypocrite if I did. She didn't know my dad was a drunk and that I would never forgive him in a million years. So how could I turn around and forgive someone I barely knew for the exact same thing?

I wished I could talk about it with her. That was the good thing about Anne-Marie. She'd known from the time we were little. The first time she came to my house, it was obvious that my dad was different. *My dad's weird*, I said, in an attempt to explain why he didn't act like other dads, and she said, *It's because of that stuff in the bottles. It makes you crazy.* And I said, *My dad is crazy every day.*

A few years later she told me my dad's craziness had a name. *It's called alky-hole-mism*, she said. *My mom told me. She said your dad is an alky-hole-lick.* I liked that it had a name. I liked that Anne-Marie was the one who told me.

I wanted Caroline to know the same way Anne-Marie knew, without me having to announce it. So I invited her to my house. After an afternoon spent ice-skating, we went back to my house for supper. Dad greeted us wearing a Santa hat and a deranged smile.

"Dad," I said. "It's not even December."

He ignored me and shook Caroline's hand. "I am ever so pleased to meet you," he boomed.

He was speaking with a British accent.

"Come in, come in," he said. "How about a nice cup of tea? It's frightfully cold outside."

Mom pushed herself in front of Dad as if she could hide him. "It's nice to meet you, Caroline. Come in and I'll take your coat."

We sat in the living room listening to Dad tell us what a dreadful time he'd had putting a spare tire on the car after it went flat in the supermarket car park. He told us it was a most harrowing experience, considering the poor weather conditions, and the worst part was when he couldn't open the boot. I felt like I was talking to Mr. Adams. He went on and on and on, then asked us to please excuse him while he went to the loo. That's when I made my escape and took Caroline to the den to hang out.

"You never told me your dad was British."

I could have told her then. The accent could have been the icebreaker. But I chickened out. "Oh yeah, that. I'm so used to it, I guess I just forgot."

"This is a cool room."

"Yeah, Iggy fixed it up for me."

"He is so cute, by the way. You never told me he was such a hottie."

"Gross! That's my uncle you're talking about."

"Tell me all about him," she said. "What's he like?"

It was nice to have someone to brag about. I showed off his university degrees and dug out his blueprints of cargo vessels and oil tankers. I showed her the books about the hydroelasticity of ships and about structural design and marine hydrodynamics, the books that made me feel like I was in a home where smart people knew stuff, where people were going somewhere. I talked about Iggy until Mom called us to the table for supper.

It was a nice civilized dinner for a while, but halfway through the meat pie Dad shouted, "Let's have a shing-along!"

This is it, I thought. *Now she'll know.*

"Oh, Phonse, we can't have a sing-along now," Mom said, as if sing-alongs were an everyday occurrence at our house. "It's time to eat."

"But it's Chrishmish!" he yelled.

"No, it's not," I said through gritted teeth.

"Sure it is!" He burst into song. "*Shilver bellsh, shilver bellsh, it's Chrishmash time in the shitty…*"

He started another. "*Have yourshelf a merry little Chrishmash…*" He flung his arms into the air, sending some glasses crashing to the floor. I was horrified but relieved at the same time. The secret was out. Now Caroline would know, just like Anne-Marie.

Caroline stood up. "Maybe I should go," she said.

"No, don't," I said. "Stay."

Iggy grabbed Dad's arm. "Come on, Phonse, let's go out for a walk. Get some fresh air."

"Right you are, my good man," said Dad. "Shplendid idear."

Iggy took Dad outside, leaving Mom, Caroline and me looking at each other in silence. Then we all said, "I'm sorry" at the same time—Mom to me, me to Caroline, and Caroline to us both. Each of us gave a nervous little laugh.

When Mom went to the kitchen to get the broom, I spoke. "My dad's a drunk."

"Yeah. I figured that out."

"And he's not British."

"I figured that out too."

We sat in silence.

"Well, I should go."

I wondered if I'd lost my only friend in St. John's.

We said goodbye on the front step.

Caroline wrapped her scarf around her neck. "See you tomorrow?"

"Really?"

"Um, yeah. Why are you so surprised?"

"Because my dad…he's an idiot."

"But you're not."

I smiled.

"So see you tomorrow?" she said.

"Definitely."

"Christmas shopping?"

I laughed. "It's a bit early, isn't it?"

"Early?" said Caroline. "No way! After all, it is Chrishmash time in the shitty."

We laughed so hard and loud that Mr. Adams opened his side window and told us to shut the bloody hell up.

DAD CAME BACK from his walk with Iggy and passed out on the couch. I waited for him to wake up. As soon as he opened his eyes, I attacked.

"When are you going to quit drinking?"

"What?"

"Drinking. When are you going to stop?"

"I'm not doing this right now, Kitty."

"Why? Do you have other plans? Going to get a drink, are you? Must be hours since your last one, you poor thing."

"Don't talk to me like that."

"Don't sing stupid drunken Christmas carols to my friends."

"I was in a good mood, that's all."

"You were drunk."

"That's enough, Kitty, I don't have to listen to this."

He started to leave the room.

"I hate you," I said quietly.

"You don't mean that."

He waited for a response. But I didn't give him one. I just stared at him until he turned around and walked away.

FOR TWO WEEKS straight, the poems showed up daily. I had to hand it to Elliot: he was really trying. And when I found "The Best Poem Ever" taped to the inside of my science binder, I knew it was time to forgive him. Because, actually, it was the *worst* poem ever, and I spent the entire period trying not to laugh.

I blew my chance
Of romance at the dance
By being a boozer
A liquored-up loser
I don't blame you for leavin'
When I started heavin'
Upchucking and spewing
Is no way of wooing
But I have paid dearly
Been punished severely
Nauseous for days

In a hung-over haze
I was death's doorish ill
But suckier still
Is the fact that you hate me
And might never date me
But I hope that this ditty
Will change your mind, Kitty
Cuz this poem's for you
And all of it's true

I didn't avoid him at our next writing group. In fact, I sought him out, waiting for him afterward outside the classroom. He looked surprised.

"You're usually long gone by now," he said. "Like a bat outta hell."

I held up the poem. He blushed.

"Suckiest thing I've ever read," I said.

"Suckiest thing I've ever written."

"Well, it worked."

"It did?"

"You get a second chance, Moptop."

His face lit up.

"But that's it. I don't do thirds."

"You won't need to," he said. "Promise."

"Good."

He smiled. "So are you going to say it?"

"Say what?"

"You know…those three little words?"

"It's a bit early for that, isn't it?"

"No, the other ones. You know, the thing you say after you accept someone's apology?"

I rolled my eyes. "Fine," I said. "I forgive you. There, I said it. I. Forgive. You."

He took both my hands in his. I got really nervous and started rambling. "But if you start going on about prisoners and forgiveness and being set free, I might reverse my decision."

He beamed. I could have dived into his dimples, they were so deep. And his eyes…it was like they were dancing.

"I won't say a word, Kit. Promise."

We stood there, just looking at each other. His hands were soft. It was awkward and lovely at the same time. "Want to go to a movie?" he asked. "Tomorrow night?"

I nodded. "Yeah, okay."

"Great."

More staring. "I think the bell might ring soon," I said.

"Yeah, I should probably head back to school," he said, but he didn't let go of my hands.

I was wondering if he was going to kiss me when I saw Amanda Shea walking toward us.

"What's wrong?" asked Elliot. "Looks like you've seen a ghost."

"It's Amanda," I whispered. "And she's coming this way."

"So?"

"So, she's probably going to have a fit."

Elliot rolled his eyes. "Who cares?"

Amanda came up behind him. "You've certainly lowered your standards, Elliot."

"Actually, I raised them," he said.

She made a noise as if she was choking and then stomped off in a huff.

Elliot smiled at me. "See? That wasn't so bad, was it?"

"I guess not. But I have to share a homeroom with her. And she hates me enough already. She thinks I'm a stupid baygirl."

He squeezed my hands. "You may be a baygirl, but you're definitely not stupid."

"And you may be a townie, but you're definitely not a snob."

He rubbed the tops of my hands with his thumbs. "The baygirl and the townie, a love story."

I laughed. "Sounds like a movie."

"We're a modern-day Romeo and Juliet," he said.

The bell rang. Elliot leaned in slowly, and my heart raced. But he didn't kiss me; he just touched the tip of my nose with his. It was the most adorable thing ever. "Bye, Kit."

"Bye, Moptop."

I floated from chemistry to math and from math to art, and after school I floated all the way to Iggy's.

Mr. Adams poked his head out his front door. "How was school, lass?"

I looked at my watch. Three fifteen on the nose, like clockwork.

"It was great!" I said.

He looked surprised. Suspicious, even. "Really?"

"Really."

Mr. Adams pumped his fist in the air like he'd just scored the winning goal in a football game. I think he might have even raised his heels a tiny bit in an attempt to jump.

And it was weird and surprising, but my eyes filled with tears. A fist pump. Just because I had a good day at school.

And things got even better when I got home and Mom told me that Ms. Bartlett had pulled some strings and got Mom her job back. *And* there was a small parcel on the kitchen table with my name on it. I opened it up. Turkish delight. Ms. Bartlett strikes again. I popped a piece of the chewy candy into my mouth and thought of Elliot. Things were looking up.

AT THE MOVIES on Friday night, Elliot held my hand from the trailer to the credits. Our palms got real sweaty, but he didn't seem to mind. Every so often he'd let go to wipe his hand down the leg of his jeans and then he'd take my hand again. He took me downtown afterward. We walked on the harborfront and looked at the boats. A cruise ship had docked for the night. It was massive, the biggest ship I'd ever seen. A sailor on a Portuguese fishing vessel whistled at me. I laughed and said, "Creepy!" But Elliot didn't find it funny at all. He put his arm around me, scowled at the guy and muttered, "I should punch his lights out." We walked along George Street, passing groups of laughing, singing, tipsy people. Live fiddle music danced out from Bridie Molloy's, and Elliot performed a spur-of-the-moment jig on the doorstep. I cracked up.

We went up Duckworth Street, where the shops were decorated with multicolored Christmas lights and people bustled by with bags full of holiday treasures.

"I'm gonna get you something really special for Christmas," Elliot said.

"You are?"

"Yep."

I started to think about what I could get him.

"Let's go in here," he said. I looked in the window of the kind of coffee shop we don't have in Parsons Bay. Modern light fixtures hung low from the ceiling over dark wooden tables. One wall was brick, and the others were painted a deep red. It looked warm and inviting.

A blast of warm air and the hiss of espresso machines greeted us as we opened the door and went inside.

"Wow, this place is blocked," I said.

At Cathy's Café and Corner Shop back home, you'd only ever see a handful of people, usually men in coveralls and old women in flowery dresses. But here, everyone was wearing trendy black clothing and carrying hip messenger bags. They were sipping drinks I'd never heard of and talking with so much expression I wanted to pull up a chair and hang on to every word. I'd never seen so many amazing people in one room.

"Um, hello?" said Elliot, waving a hand in front of my face. "Anyone home?"

"Um, excuse me? Can I help you?" I said. "You're interrupting my people-watching."

"So why don't you watch me instead?"

"I'm not sure you're interesting enough," I said. "No piercings, no tattoos…not that I can see anyway."

"Well, we'll let that remain a mystery, shall we?" he said, reaching across the table and taking my hands. "For now anyway."

We ordered hot chocolate and talked for ages. He told me about his grandfather and I told him about Nan. We talked about our next writing-group assignment. We had to write a poem about a special object, and Elliot said he was going to write about his grandpa's pocket watch.

I had been so busy trying to think of my own special object that I hadn't thought of borrowing someone else's.

I told him all about Parsons Bay. He got a great kick out of Fisty Hinks.

"Why do you call him Fisty?" he asked.

"Because every time a kid went on his property or made a racket in front of his house, he stuck his fist out the door and shook it."

Elliot laughed. "Just his fist? Did he ever stick his face out? Did he ever say anything?"

"That depended on how fast you could run past his house."

"What do you mean?"

"Well, the little kids who couldn't run very fast got the whole Fisty on the doorstep, complete with the fist shake and the *I'll getcha, ya little buggers.* Older kids got just the sight of his arm and fist sticking through the door and an *I'll getcha, ya lit* and some really fast runners got just the fist with an *I'll getch.* Janice Dooley, who was the fastest runner in town, was lucky enough to get by with just the knuckles and an *I'll.*"

Elliot was killing himself laughing. "What about if you were older?"

"Oh, kids over fourteen didn't run at all—they just moseyed by and pretended they weren't scared at all, but if you watched real close, you would see their steps quicken when Fisty appeared."

Elliot took my hand. "You're hysterical."

When we'd drained our drinks, we strolled home from downtown. As Elliot walked me to my front door, snow started to fall. It was like a scene from a romantic movie.

"Well, see ya," I said.

"Yeah, see ya."

Neither of us moved.

"I should go in now, Moptop."

"Okay. Bye."

We stood staring at each other.

"Well, this is awkward," I said.

Elliot leaned in, so I swallowed quickly and closed my eyes. And then it happened. It finally happened. He kissed me. His lips were unbelievably soft.

"Bye," he whispered.

I turned to go in, and as I reached for the doorknob, I caught Mr. Adams watching me from his side window. The moment we locked eyes, he looked away.

That night I wrote Anne-Marie another letter. Three pages. About Elliot. And as I addressed the envelope carefully and neatly, I hoped that this time I'd get one in return.

AFTER THAT FIRST kiss, Elliot and I were inseparable. I no longer spent lunchtime alone in the cloakroom. Instead, I'd meet Elliot at a hamburger joint not far from school.

We'd buy a couple of drinks, so we couldn't be accused of loitering, and stay there for most of the hour, holding hands across the table and talking. We'd meet again at three and hang out until suppertime, walking through the streets of downtown or sharing a tin of drink and a kiss behind Pelley's. The only afternoon I didn't spend with Elliot was cleaning day at Mr. Adams's. He told me he'd missed seeing me walk past his house on my way home from school and asked what I'd been up to.

"You mean you don't already know?" I asked as I wiped down his kitchen counter.

Mr. Adams settled in at the kitchen table. "Why would I?"

I nodded toward his side window. "Well, you seem to have a front-row seat to my life."

Mr. Adams startled me with a big guffaw. "Ha!" he shrieked, slapping the table with the palm of his hand.

"It's not funny," I said. "Why are you asking something you already know the answer to?"

Mr. Adams folded his arms and narrowed his eyes. "To see if you'd 'fess up, lass."

It was my turn to burst out laughing. "*'Fess up*?"

"Aye. 'Fess up."

I threw my cleaning rag under the sink. "It's not a crime to have a boyfriend, you know."

"It's a crime to my eyes," said Mr. Adams. "Canoodling like that in public."

I hid a smirk. "There are these things called curtains, you know. Not only do they open but they also close."

"'Ave your parents met him?" he asked.

"No." I snorted. "If he gets any farther than the door-step, I might never see him again."

"You embarrassed of him then?"

"No! Why would I be? He's smart and gorgeous and funny and—"

"I meant your father, lass."

"Oh. Well, yeah, obviously. He's an idiot."

"Well, you can't hide your young man forever, you know."

"You're one to talk," I said. "You kept Elspeth away from your family."

"Aye, I did, flower. Like I said before, they were cold to her. But your family might like your fella. You won't know unless you introduce 'em."

I shrugged. "Maybe."

"Invite the lad over at Christmas," Mr. Adams suggested. "Everyone's jolly at Christmas."

What the hell, I thought. I called Elliot that night and invited him to come over on Christmas Eve. He said yes straightaway. I, on the other hand, was having second thoughts. Mr. Adams was right. Everyone *is* jolly at Christmas. The problem was, my father's holiday cheer came in a bottle.

SIX
The Mystery Gift

On Christmas Eve, when Dad heard I had a friend coming over, he put his bottle of rum back in the liquor cabinet. Mom and Iggy exchanged glances when they saw him pour himself a Pepsi, straight up, but said nothing. I guess they didn't want to jinx it.

Iggy put up the Christmas tree he'd bought in the Canadian Tire parking lot that morning, and once it was positioned just so, at an angle we could all agree on, we realized we had no decorations. Iggy had given his to the Salvation Army, along with his furniture, and ours were in a box in Parsons Bay, hidden away in Nan's basement.

"Popcorn!" Iggy said. "We can string popcorn! And cranberries!" We strung popcorn and cranberries until the Christmas tree looked only slightly more festive than Charlie Brown's.

Mom filled every inch of the coffee table with snacks: mini sausage rolls, chunks of cheese on toothpicks, ham sandwiches cut into little triangles and big bowls full of pretzels and chips. She also filled a three-tier cake plate with Christmas cake and shortbread cookies. Iggy put on Bing Crosby's *White Christmas* and built a fire in the fireplace. It was the same old room with the same old people, but somehow Christmas always managed to make things feel different and special. Perfect, almost. Except that Nan wasn't there. Ms. Bartlett had called and said Nan had a cold and wasn't up to traveling. She said not to worry; they'd have a nice Christmas together and Nan would call on Christmas Day. I couldn't wait to talk to her.

Iggy passed me a glass of eggnog.

"You look good, Iggy," I said. He had on a green cashmere sweater and a pair of dark blue jeans.

"So do you."

Mom had given me an early Christmas present: money for a new outfit to wear over the holidays. I had bought a fitted red sweater dress, black leggings and a pair of knee-high black boots. I hoped Elliot would like it.

I nibbled on pretzels while I waited for the doorbell to ring.

"Do you like him then?" asked Iggy.

I felt my face flush. "Who, Elliot?"

"Yeah, she likes him," teased Dad. "Just look at her face. It's red as a beet."

Mom laughed.

I threw a cushion at Iggy and went to the front door to peek out. As I scanned the street up and down, looking for Elliot, I caught sight of Mr. Adams sitting at his kitchen table, staring at his teapot. A wave of sadness rushed through me, and my heart felt three sizes too small, just like the Grinch's. I went back to the living room.

"Would it be okay if I invited Mr. Adams over?" I asked.

"Sure!" said Iggy. "The more the merrier!"

Mr. Adams looked touched when I asked him to join us. I helped him into his coat and, linking my arm through his, walked him over to Iggy's. While the adults sat in the living room chatting, I waited.

It was nine thirty when the doorbell rang.

Elliot was out of breath. "Sorry I'm late. We had company drop by and I couldn't leave."

I hugged him. "Doesn't matter. You're here now."

Elliot was wearing a shirt and tie, dressed to impress. And I could tell by the way the adults looked at him that it had worked. He shook their hands and introduced himself, and when he got to Mom, he added a kiss on the cheek that made her go all giggly and schoolgirlish.

"So," said Mr. Adams, "this must be the lad you were playin' tonsil tennis with the other night, eh?"

I closed my eyes. "Oh. My. God."

Elliot tried to speak. "We were just…I mean, I was just…I mean, it was just…I really like Kit and…"

Mom sat on the arm of Dad's chair. "Young love, hey, Phonse?"

He took her hand. "I remember it well."

Iggy passed Elliot a drink and asked him about school. Iggy had gone to the same one, so they settled on the couch and sank into a deep discussion about which teachers were still there and how the sports teams were doing and other stuff that was boring to everyone but them.

Mom and Mr. Adams hit it off too. She was having a great time listening to his Yorkshire stories. They spoke about me as well. I heard him say he was "very fond" of me, despite my "impertinence." Mom asked if he'd like to come for Christmas dinner. His eyes lit up. "Did Thomas Crapper invent the toilet?" Mom didn't get that he meant yes and said she didn't know. Mr. Adams laughed. "He was from Yorkshire, you know." Then he launched into a long list of amazing historical figures "birthed by his home-land." Mom nodded her head throughout the speech and tried to look impressed.

Dad was quiet at first, but by the end of the night he was singing along to the CD and had everyone joining in.

He danced my mother around the room and almost knocked over the Christmas tree. It was clear the stuff in the bottle had somehow made its way into his Pepsi. No one except me seemed to mind.

At the end of the night, when Elliot and Mr. Adams had gone home, Dad knocked on my door. I was sitting on my bed, doing some last-minute wrapping.

"Your young man's a fine fellow," he said.

"Yeah, he is."

"That went well, don't you think?"

He was fishing for compliments. Proud of himself for not putting on a show. Well, as he would say, whoopdi-bloody-doo. What did he want? A medal? I wasn't about to give him any compliments for acting halfway normal for once in his life.

"It was okay," I said flatly.

He just stood there, like a little boy waiting for approval.

"Was there anything else you wanted?"

He shook his head.

"Okay, well, I have some presents to wrap."

He nodded and, with slumped shoulders, left the room.

IGGY BANGED ON my door Christmas morning. "Get up, get up!"

Bleary-eyed, I opened my door. "What are you, five? Sheesh! It's seven AM!"

"There are presents under the tree!"

"Well, yeah. It *is* Christmas morning."

"Come on!" he said, pulling on my arm. "Let's go!"

Mom and Dad sat sleepily on the couch.

"He's insane," grumbled Dad.

Mom smiled. "You were always the first one up when we were little, weren't you, Ig?"

Iggy sat down by the tree. "Enough talking. Let's get these opened! I'll be Santa."

He passed each of us a gift. "These ones are from me."

My gift was a beautiful wooden jewelry box. Now if only I had some jewelry to put in it.

We spent the next half hour opening gifts—gifts from me to them (mostly chocolates and sweets from Pelley's because I couldn't afford much else), gifts from Mom and Dad to Iggy and me, and gifts sent from Parsons Bay. There weren't a lot of expensive gifts in the pile, but, as the old saying goes, it's the thought that counts, and it was clear that a lot of thought had been put into each one of them.

While Mom and Iggy started the turkey preparations, I talked to Nan on the phone. Her voice was all croaky. When it was Dad's turn to talk, I knelt by the tree, eating a candy cane and examining my presents. That's when I noticed an unopened one, tucked in close to the tree stand. It was a small box in plaid wrapping paper, and it had my name on it. I opened it. My heart almost stopped. It was the bracelet.

The bracelet from Pelley's. Elliot must have slipped it under the tree the night before. I put it on. It was gorgeous.

Mom admired it during dinner. "It's lovely," she said. "Elliot has good taste."

After dessert, I phoned him. "Meet me behind Pelley's."

As soon as I saw him, I hugged him. "Thank you, Moptop! I love it!"

"Love what?"

I held up my wrist. "The bracelet."

"Well, this is awkward," he said.

"What?"

"I didn't buy you that bracelet."

"Oh." I was confused. My mind raced, searching for an explanation. Then I slapped myself on the forehead. "I'm so dumb. The bracelet must be from Iggy!" I said. "He gave me a jewelry box. This must go with it!"

"That makes sense."

"I'm so embarrassed."

"Don't be," he said. "No big deal. I do have a gift for you though."

"You do?"

"Yep. Wanna see it?"

I nodded.

He took a small gift-wrapped box out of his pocket.

My hands shook slightly as I opened it.

"It's amethyst," he said.

I slid the gold ring with the purple stone on my finger. "I love it."

"I'm glad."

I reached into the inside pocket of my coat and passed him a present wrapped in gold paper. "I've got something for you too."

He tore the paper off. "Wow."

"It's a journal. For your poems and stuff."

"And it's leather too. Awesome. Thanks, Kit."

He leaned against the brick wall of the store and I leaned into him.

"Have you finished your special-object assignment?" I asked.

"Not quite. You?"

"Almost."

"Maybe we can work on them together," he said. "Your place? Tomorrow afternoon?"

I nodded.

"*Joyeux Noël*, Kit."

"Merry Christmas, Moptop."

IGGY WAS DOZING on the couch in a turkey stupor when I got home.

"Hey," I said, jostling his arm gently. "Why didn't you say this bracelet was from you?"

"What? Huh?"

"This bracelet," I said, waving my arm in front of his face. "Why didn't you say it was from you?"

He sat up and rubbed his eyes. "Because it's not."

"It's not?"

He shook his head. "Mr. Adams, maybe?"

"Maybe," I said. But I didn't think so. Mr. Adams had already given me my gift, a book called *Miss Manners' Guide to Excruciatingly Correct Behavior.* He'd said I could learn a thing or two from it. When I'd opened it, I'd wished I'd given him some smart-ass book about being old and crotchety, but I didn't know if one existed and it was too late anyway, because I'd already bought him a Lifesavers Sweet Storybook and a package of Jammy Dodgers that I'd specially ordered from Bartlett's.

That left Dad. He was in his bedroom, sitting on his bed and staring out the window. He had a drink in his hand.

"Why didn't you just say it was from you?" I asked. "Isn't that what normal people do? They write their name on the gift tag or, even better, they hand it over and say, 'Merry Christmas, this is from me.'"

"I didn't want to make a big deal out of it."

"Well, you failed. Because you've made a huge deal out of it. I've just made a fool of myself saying thank you to Elliot and then to Iggy for something neither of them gave me."

"Sorry, Kitty." He downed his drink. "I can't do anything right where you're concerned, can I?"

My heart sank. He was right.

I sat next to him and fiddled with the bracelet.

"How did you know?"

"Mr. Pelley told me."

Why was it so hard for Dad to just give it to me?

Why was it so hard for me to just say I liked it?

I took a deep breath. "I love it, Dad. I really do. Thanks."

He patted my knee awkwardly. "You're welcome, Kitty."

I got up and went to the door. "Merry Christmas, Dad."

ELLIOT AND I spent the next few days working on our special-object poems. I couldn't wait to share mine with Mr. Adams. I stood on his doorstep in the freezing cold and rang his bell. He took ages to answer it, and when he finally did, he said, "What are you doing just standing there? Come in out of the cold, you silly girl."

He made some tea, and when he stretched the tea cozy around the pot, my heart skipped a beat because that's what I'd written my poem about. The tea cozy was my special object. I couldn't wait any longer. I had to read it to him.

"Mr. Adams?"

"Aye?"

"Um, I have a poem for you."

"Lovely jubbly. Is this from that writin' class of yours?"

"Yeah, we had to write about a special object. I don't really have a special object, but I know you do, so I thought I would write about it…in your honor."

He settled in with his tea and bickies.

"Let's hear it."

I took the poem out of my back pocket and cleared my throat.

"Oh," he interrupted, "there's something I've been meanin' to tell you."

"What's that?"

"Did you know that the tallest tree in Yorkshire is a lime tree? One hundred and fifty feet tall. It's in Duncombe Park."

"Oh, that's…interesting."

"Okay," he said. "I'm ready."

I had just opened my mouth to speak when a fly appeared, landing on the side of Mr. Adams's teacup.

"Ee, will you look at that," he said. "A fly. In the middle of winter."

"Yep, it's a fly." I held up my paper and cleared my throat. "Now, my poem."

"'Ave you ever seen a Yorkshire fly? Jolly good things, Yorkshire flies."

I put my paper down and indulged him.

"Okay, tell me. What's so good about a Yorkshire fly?

And what's the difference between a Yorkshire fly and non-Yorkshire fly anyway?"

"Aha!" Mr. Adams exclaimed, as if he'd just made an amazing discovery. "A Yorkshire fly is not a livin' fly!"

"So a Yorkshire fly is a dead fly? So does that mean that all dead flies are Yorkshire flies?"

"Nay, lass. A Yorkshire fly is a fishin' fly."

"A fishing fly?"

"Aye, a fishin' fly. I've caught many a trout with the trusty Yorkshire fly. It's made with a very lightweight wire hook and just a sprinklin' of game feathers."

"Cool."

"Now then, let's get back to more important matters," Mr. Adams said, opening his door and waving goodbye to the fly. "Cheerio, old chap."

"Right," he said. "I'm ready for the poem. As you young folk say, hit me with it!"

I'd never said "hit me with it" in my life, but I cleared my throat and began.

"Object Of My Affection"
Written by Kit Ryan
For Reginald Adams

Oh, lovely, wooly tea cozy
What a warm hug you give my tea

You fill me with such glee
Wooly, warm, knit by angels
Sweet as tea itself
Your multicolored hues
Brighten my day
Every day
Without fail
Oh, lovely wooly tea cozy

I looked up from my paper. Mr. Adams was staring at the tea cozy. He looked deep in thought.

"Bloody hell." He sounded astonished. I smiled. I'd blown him away with my writing.

"I take it you like it?"

"Like it? I bloody hated it. It's bloody awful. Knit by bloody angels? Sweet as bloody tea itself? What a load of bloody rubbish."

Well. I might not have been the best writer in the world, but I knew "overuse of a word" when I heard it, and to say that Mr. Adams had just overused the word *bloody* was an understatement.

"But I thought it was a special object to you."

"A bloody tea cozy? Special?"

"Well, you use it every day."

"I use toilet paper every day too. Is that special?"

"But your wife…she knit it."

"She knit me long underwear too, but it's not my prized bloody possession." He shook his head. "A bloody tea cozy. Multicolored bloody hues. Fills me with glee, my arse."

I looked at my poem and sighed. When I wrote it, I thought it was genius. But it was clear now that it sucked. Big time.

Mr. Adams saw my disappointment. "Listen, flower. It's a tea cozy. I don't like cold tea. That's all there is to it. Now get off your arse, get yourself home, and write something good. You'll be laughed out of the class if you bring that flamin' piece of rubbish in."

"But what will I write about?"

"Think of something *really* special. Something unforgettable. Something dear to your heart. Something as unlike a bloody tea cozy as humanly possible."

He picked up my poem and shook it at me. "You're made of better stuff than this, love. Now go home and get crackin'."

ON NEW YEAR'S Eve, Mom and Dad came in and sat down on the edge of my bed. Iggy stood in the doorway, looking serious and slightly ticked off. My stomach twisted into a knot. Something was wrong.

Ms. Bartlett had called. Nan had pneumonia. She was sick with a fever, and her cough was so bad that she had trouble breathing at times. She was on antibiotics but wasn't getting any better. Mom said Dad was going back to Parsons Bay to take care of her temporarily. I could stay in St. John's or I could go back to Parsons Bay and spend time with Nan. She said it was my choice.

"What about you, Mom? Aren't you going back?"

"I have to stay here, Kit. I'm the only one with a job."

I thought about Nan. Dad would suck at looking after her by himself.

"What about school?" I asked.

"If you go back to Parsons Bay, you'll just go back to your old school," Mom said.

"I think you should come with me, Kitty," said Dad. "I'll need your help."

Iggy spoke up. "She's *your* mother, Phonse. She's not Kit's responsibility."

"This doesn't concern you, Iggy," snapped Dad.

"But she *is* my responsibility, Iggy," I said. "She's my grandmother. And she's sick. She needs me."

"You're a kid!" he barked. "Not a bloody nurse! You belong here! Not in Parsons Bay!"

"Iggy," I said, "just hear me out."

"No!" he said. "You're staying here and that's that!"

"I'm not," I said. "I can't. I mean, I should go—Nan needs me."

"Jesus, Kit," Iggy shouted. "Don't be such a martyr!"

The room fell silent. Iggy's face softened. "Kit, I—"

But I didn't want to listen anymore. Iggy reached for me as I brushed past, but I pulled away and rushed down the stairs.

"Kit, wait!"

I slammed the door to the den and sat on the couch, shaking. My father had raised his voice at me almost every day of my life, but I had never expected to hear my Uncle Iggy do the same.

I could still hear him, even with the door closed. "Okay, you want to know the truth? I don't think Kit should be living with you, Phonse. Not alone. You're a drunk. A bloody good-for-nothing drunk. You can't be trusted. Look what you did to Emily that time!"

"Mind your own goddamn business," my father yelled.

"She won't be alone," my mother said. "She'll be with her nan."

"Who is sick!" said Iggy. "Kit needs someone looking after her, not the other way around!"

"I'm sorry, Iggy," said Mom. "Kit needs to be with her nan. It might be the last chance she gets."

I felt like throwing up.

I heard footsteps on the stairs, then a knock on my door.

I wiped my eyes.

"Come in."

Iggy sat next to me. "I'm sorry. For shouting like that."

"Don't worry, Iggy. I can handle him."

"I know you can. But you shouldn't have to."

"Yeah, well, life sucks sometimes."

He sighed. "Yeah, it does."

"But we'll manage, won't we?"

Iggy put his arm around me. "Yes, yes we will."

I BANGED ON Mr. Adams's door. "I'm leaving. I have to go back to Parsons Bay. To take care of my nan."

"Very well," he said.

"Very well? That's it? That's all you have to say?"

"Bon voyage?"

I stormed out.

"I-I-I'm not very good with words," he called from his front step.

I stopped on his path. "Not good with words?" I shouted. "You don't shut up for five minutes. Your mouth runs all day long!"

"Why don't you come back in? We'll 'ave a bickie."

"Stuff your bickies!"

I went home and called Elliot, hoping he'd have a more heartfelt reaction to my news.

Telling Elliot over the phone was too hard, so we met behind Pelley's. When I told him I was leaving, he cried.

He actually cried. He tried to hide it by pulling up his hood, but I could hear him sniffing, and when he finally looked up his eyes were red.

I cried too. But I didn't hide it. Elliot wiped my cheeks with his sleeve.

"What a way to start the new year," he said.

"I know. But if it was your grandpa, you'd go too, wouldn't you?"

"Absolutely."

"So you understand?"

"Yeah. But I'm really going to miss you."

"Will you come visit?"

Elliot put his arm around me. "As often as I can. I promise."

I put my head on his chest.

"I love you," I said.

It came out. Just like that.

I waited for him to say something.

He didn't.

I wished I could take a great big breath and suck the words right back into my mouth.

I tilted my head up slightly to take a peek at his face.

He was grinning.

"*Je t'aime aussi.*"

WITHIN DAYS WE were packed and ready to go. The day we were to leave St. John's, I went back to Mr. Adams's house.

"Can we have a proper goodbye now?" I asked.

"I'm happy you came back, lass. Come in and I'll put the kettle on."

"I brought my poem," I said. "New and improved."

We sat at the kitchen table.

"Let's hear it," he said. "Special object. Round two. This better be good."

I reached into my knapsack for my paper.

"Wait just a tick," Mr. Adams said, jumping up from his chair to look out the window. "Look, a Yorkshire terrier. Crackin' good dog. The best there is, in my opinion. You can keep your bloody retrievers and shepherds. The Yorkshire terrier, that's the dog for me."

He sat back down, coughing, sputtering and gasping as if the act of getting up to look out the window had almost killed him. He beat on his chest with his fist. "Remember, one lung. Don't forget what I said about the lung."

"You never said anything about having one lung."

Mr. Adams ignored me. He did one more heaving cough and looked up at a crucifix hanging over his kitchen door. "God help me, me and my one lung."

I waited patiently.

"Okeydokey," he said chirpily. "Special object, poem number two. Hit me with it."

I really did want to hit him with it. I wanted to roll my paper up into a tube and give him a smack on his crotchety old noggin, but I didn't. I cleared my throat.

"*Reginald," written by Kit Ryan.*

"What did you just say?" he interrupted. "Reginald? Is this poem about me? Am I the bloody object? Do I look like a bloody object to you? I am a livin', breathin' human being, not a flamin' inanimate object."

"I just wanted to write about something—well, I guess I mean *someone* special."

Mr. Adams looked surprised. "Oh, well, right you are, then. Special, aye, certainly. Okay then, let's hear it."

"Reginald"
Written by Kit Ryan
For Reginald Adams

A cliff,
Battered by wind and sea
Changes its shape
Weathered
But not weakened
Strong as ever
He is like that
A man,
Battered by judgment

His choices challenged
Weathered
But not weakened
Strong as ever
Morals formed
By hardship
Every crack
Every crevice
Filled
With what is right
And what is true
He is a cliff
Eroded
But solid
Strong as ever

I placed my poem on the table and looked up. Mr. Adams took a sip of tea and cleared his throat. "Ee, I'll tell you one thing," he said. "It's a damn sight better than that tea cozy rubbish."

"Thanks."

He got up and went to the window. "And *eroded but solid? Cracks and crevices?* You make me sounds like a right decrepit old fart." He paused a moment. "It's not bad though…if you like that sort of sentimental rubbish."

He looked at his watch. "It's getting late. You'll be heading out soon."

I got up to leave. "I'll miss you, Mr. Adams."

"Yes, yes, I know you will."

I was surprised by the stinging I felt in my eyes. "Ee by gum," I said. "I feel like I might cry."

"Your bladder is too near your eyes, you silly girl."

I gave him a hug. "Well, bye."

"Okay, okay, flower," he said, patting my back. "Cheerio and ta-ra and all that rubbish."

So I left. And as I walked down the front path of Yorkshire Cottage, I looked back and saw, through the window, Mr. Adams reading my poem.

WE DROVE ACROSS the province in our old Buick, the flatbed trailer hitched once again to the back, with Dad's smelly old recliner on top. I sat in the backseat and opened my goodbye presents: writing paper and a book of stamps from Caroline, a necklace with a heart charm from Elliot, an envelope of money from Iggy and the multicolored knitted tea cozy from Mr. Adams.

The drive seemed longer this time. Maybe because Mom wasn't there making small talk. I purposely sat in the back to annoy my dad, and, as I predicted, he worked himself into a tizzy about how he wasn't my bloody chauffeur and who did I think I was, Princess Bloody Di? When his rant was over, the car was filled with an awkward silence.

We drove though the outskirts of St. John's. Large car lots and industrial buildings provided a bit of visual stimulation, but once we hit the Trans-Canada Highway, everything looked the same. The road was smooth, but the terrain that surrounded it was barren and rough. The landscape was mostly fir and birch trees, but every so often changed to scrubland, boggy and bare. To tourists it was probably rugged and rustic, majestic almost, but to me it was boring as hell. So, as I had on our last journey across the province, I slept.

We stopped at an Irving restaurant for lunch. I ate a grilled-cheese sandwich alone at the counter while Dad sat in a booth and talked to some truckers. Soon we were back on the road, and when Dad slowed to take Route 320, I sat up straight and opened the window. We were only an hour away. Dad whistled as we wound our way along the Kittiwake Coast, in and out of tiny fishing villages, until we reached the one that mattered most: Parsons Bay.

Walking into Nan's house was like slipping on a pair of favorite slippers. Warm and inviting. I tried to hide my shock when I saw her. She was stooped and small and pale. Like a little white ghost. She said she was sorry to cause us so much trouble. Dad said it was no trouble at all and how about a cup of tea, but he made no move to put the kettle on, so I did. I helped Nan into her rocker and tucked a blanket around her. I added honey to the tea instead of sugar because I knew it was good for coughs. When I stretched the tea cozy around the pot, I told Nan that it was a gift from a friend of mine. And then I told her all about Mr. Adams. "I'd like to meet him someday," she said.

When Nan got tired, I put her to bed. I went back to the kitchen and made homemade bread, just like Nan had taught me. The first step was activating the yeast by mixing it with warm water and sugar. Within minutes the mixture had turned frothy, a guarantee of nicely risen bread. After mixing in the flour, water, butter and salt to form a soft dough, I turned it out onto Nan's lightly floured table. Then I started to knead it just the way she had showed me, folding the dough in on itself, pushing it out with the heel of my hand, then rotating it a quarter-turn and starting again. When it had transformed from a wet blob into beautiful, smooth dough, I placed it in a bowl and covered it with a tea towel. Then I sat alone at her kitchen table and waited for my favorite part—punching down the risen dough, shaping it into loaves and waiting for it to rise again. Nan said the key to good breadmaking was patience. So I settled into a kitchen chair and relaxed.

I looked out at the Atlantic and listened to *The Fisheries Broadcast* on Nan's transistor radio. I was home.

BEFORE I WENT to see Anne-Marie, I went by my old house. I was surprised by how little emotion I felt seeing my old home boarded up and empty. Nan's house felt more like home. And, strangely enough, so did Iggy's.

Out of habit, I ran past Fisty Hinks's even though I was pretty sure he'd moved in with Ms. Bartlett. When I reached Anne-Marie's house, I threw a handful of pebbles at her window. A moment later she was standing on her front step, in a pair of tight jeans and a fitted tank top.

"Wow! Look at you!" I said.

She put her hands on her hips and posed like she was a supermodel.

"What can I say?"

"You can say you missed me."

"I pined for you the whole time," she said, wiping away an invisible tear. "Why, I haven't slept a wink in six months just thinking about you."

I rolled my eyes. "Yeah, right."

"What's with the pebbles?" she asked. "You haven't done that since we were eight."

"I know." I laughed. "I did it for old times' sake."

She smiled. "I'm really glad you're back."

"Come here, you."

We hugged.

Something was different.

"Are you wearing perfume?"

She raised her eyebrows and gave a sly smile. "Chanel Number Five. Toby loves it."

"Toby? Toby Burt? Are you and he…?"

She pulled on a pair of boots and grabbed a purse. "C'mon. Let's go to our spot. I got lots to tell you."

Mounds of dirty snow were dotted here and there like giant burnt marshmallows. It took longer than usual to get to the top of the cliff because Anne-Marie's high-heeled boots kept getting stuck in the ground. We found two boulders to sit on and faced the cliff's edge. The ocean breeze had a cold edge and brought with it misty droplets that left our cheeks shiny and red.

"I've missed this," I said.

Anne-Marie pulled her scarf up over her face. "It's friggin' freezing."

"I love it." I took a breath so deep, I snorted.

Anne-Marie laughed. "Manners, Kit. Remember what Ms. Bartlett used to say—*learn manners now so when you're big, you won't be called a big fat pig.*"

I pushed the tip of my nose up with my finger and snorted again and again until Anne-Marie pushed me off my boulder.

"Come on, tell me all the gossip," I said, brushing bits of snow off my pants.

"Well, the biggest news is that Ms. Bartlett got married. To Fisty Hinks!"

"Yeah, I know. Nan told me. I can't picture it."

"I know. It's *so* weird."

"So is she Mrs. Hinks now?"

"Nah," said Anne-Marie. "I asked her and she said *Getting married does not mean giving up your identity.*"

I laughed. "That is so Ms. Bartlett."

"Totally."

"Anyway," I said, elbowing Anne-Marie in the ribs, "enough about her love life. What's this about you and Toby?"

Anne-Marie's eyes lit up. "We've been going out for two months, three weeks and two days."

"Really? So what's he like?"

"He's cool and nice and cute. It's different from when we were kids—you know what I mean? He's mature now. He's sensitive."

"So how did it happen? How did you hook up?"

She told me everything about him. "It was a Friday night, and everyone was hanging out on the cliff. I couldn't get my bag of salt-and-vinegar chips open, so Toby opened them with his teeth. When he passed them back, I said, *Ewww, this bag's got your spit on it now,* and he said, *Doesn't matter, we'll be swapping spit later tonight anyway.* I swear, Kit, it was the most romantic thing I'd ever heard."

It sounded kind of gross to me, but I said nothing.

"And you should see his face when he says *I love you*— it goes all red. Totally adorable. And his eyebrows do this thing where they rise every time he takes a drag on his cigarette. It's so cute. I'm telling you, Kit, he's simply perfect."

I looked out at the ocean and pulled the neck of my shirt up over my nose, smelling the perfume that had rubbed off when we hugged. I wondered if Elliot would like me to wear Chanel N° 5.

"I was in a daze the first few weeks of going out with Toby," Anne-Marie continued. "I even forgot to eat!"

I tugged my shirt down off my nose. "Really? I'd never forget to eat. I like food too much."

Anne-Marie put her hand on my shoulder. "Trust me, Kit. When *you're* in love, you'll know exactly what I mean."

"But I *am* in love. Remember? The letter I sent? I told you all about him."

"Oh, right. What was his name again?"

"Elliot. I call him Moptop, remember?"

She burst out laughing. "Moptop? What kind of nick-name is that?"

I shrugged her hand off my shoulder.

"It's a nickname. His hair…it's curly. It was all in the letter."

"Oh, I remember now," she said, playfully slapping my leg. "What's he like?"

Suddenly I didn't feel like telling her every detail.

"He's really smart. He likes to speak French."

She giggled. "A nerd, huh?"

I felt myself flush. I tried to think of something to tell her. Something awesome about Elliot.

"Does he play sports?" she asked. "Toby plays on five teams." She counted on her fingers. "Soccer, lacrosse, hockey, football and…let me see, there's one more…um…"

When Elliot had tried to play basketball with Iggy in the driveway, he was hopeless. He'd dribble the ball and his curls would fall into his eyes, and he was constantly blowing air upward out of his mouth, desperate to get the hair out of his face. And on every attempt at a basket, he'd stick his tongue out in concentration. And I found all of these things "simply perfect."

"Basketball!" Anne-Marie exclaimed. "That's the one. Basketball. Toby's the star player."

I picked up a stone and threw it over the cliff's edge.

"So tell me more about St. John's," she said.

"Not much to tell."

"There must be something."

There were lots of somethings. Days' and days' worth.

"Did you make any friends?"

"Um, yeah. Didn't you read my letters?"

"Of course I did. It was a long time ago, that's all. Refresh my memory."

"There is this old man next door, and he's really eccentric and—"

"An old man? Are you serious? You made friends with some kooky old geezer?"

"Well, he, um, he needed someone to clean and—"

"Oh. My. God. Do *not* tell me you were somebody's cleaner. Gross."

It had only been six months, but the girl in the paint-spattered overalls was gone.

"Did you manage to meet anyone your own age or what?"

"Yeah. A girl in my class. Caroline. We got pretty close."

Anne-Marie took a compact mirror out of her purse and examined her face.

"So? What's she like?"

"Well, she's into grunge."

"Grunge?"

"Yeah, you know, like Nirvana and Green Day?"

Anne-Marie put on some lipstick and puckered, admiring her handiwork. "Never heard of them."

"She's into carpentry too. She even started a petition to get a shop class started at our school. And she's super sporty. Star of the floor-hockey team and everything."

Anne-Marie snapped the compact shut. "Ooooh, gotta watch out for those sporty types. Lesbians."

I looked at Anne-Marie like she had ten heads. "That's ridiculous."

"It's true. Toby said that he went to a co-ed hockey camp last summer and most of the girls there were dykes. This Caroline chick's probably a lesbo with the hots for you."

I shielded my eyes from the nonexistent sun.

"She actually reminded me of you," I said quietly.

"Really? Weird. Anyway, sorry to cut this short, but I gotta go. I'm meeting Toby. For some QT—you know, quality time? See you at school on Monday?"

"Yup."

She stood up to go. "Just so you know, you might think about dressing up a bit. For school. We kind of go all out now, you know what I mean?"

I picked some lint off my brown cords. "Yeah, sure."

"We're cool, right, Kit?"

"Yeah, sure."

"See ya later then?"

"Yup."

"You staying here?"

"Yup."

"Suit yourself. Laters."

She left me on the cliff's edge, longing for the nerd, the so-called dyke and the kooky old geezer. I pulled the neck of my shirt up over my nose again. Barely a trace of Chanel N° 5 remained.

MY FATHER SAT around drinking all day long and did nothing to help Nan. I didn't mind tending to Nan, but tending to Dad really pissed me off. I made sure he knew it too. At lunch I'd carefully place Nan's meal in front of her, but I'd practically throw my dad's at him. At supper I'd give Nan the nicest pieces of meat, and I'd give Dad all the burnt bits. And at bedtime I'd fluff Nan's pillow and give her extra blankets, but I'd turn the lights out on my father, leaving him to sleep it off in his recliner, cold and uncomfortable.

Ms. Bartlett had a fit one day when she came to check on things. She took one look at me and tore into my father. "The girl's exhausted. Can't you see that?"

"What do you want me to do about it?" he said. "I can't cook. I can't do all that woman's stuff."

"Then why did you bother coming back to Parsons Bay? You're just a hindrance here. You're making it harder for Kit."

Dad poured himself a drink. "Why don't you mind your own business and go plant a tree or something, you big hippie."

I exploded. "Why don't you shut the hell up? Ms. Bartlett's only trying to help."

Nan called out from the bedroom.

"Nice one, Kitty," said Dad. "Now look what you did. You woke her."

I shot him a look and made a move to go see to Nan.

"I'll go," said Ms. Bartlett. "Sit down, Kit, and put your feet up."

When Ms. Bartlett had left the room, Dad smirked at me. I could have smacked him. Instead, I smirked back, and then I picked up his bottle of booze and threw it against the wall, just like he did with the bowl of beans all those years ago. The glass smashed into a million pieces and the stinky, disgusting liquid sprayed everywhere, and I wanted to sop it up with a sponge and rub it hard into his ugly face and say, "Here ya go, Dad, here's your booze. Are ya happy now?"

I thought I was as mad as I could get, but when Dad didn't react, I got even madder.

"Guess you'll be running down to the liquor store to replace that," he said calmly.

"In your dreams!"

Ms. Bartlett ran into the room. "What on earth?"

She took one look at me, shaking with anger amidst a sea of shattered glass, and understood. She grabbed Dad's coat from the hook in the hallway and threw it at him. "Go," she said. "Give us all a break for a while and get out."

"Fine." He shrugged. "No sweat off my back. I'll go down to the pub."

I rolled my eyes. "Surprise! Sur-freakin'-surprise!"

Dad got up from his chair. "Sarcasm doesn't suit you, Kitty."

"And drinking doesn't suit you."

He went to the front door. "You always have to have the last word, don't you?"

"Yep."

He opened the door.

"Don't let the door hit ya where the good Lord split ya," I said as he went through it.

Ms. Bartlett and I burst out laughing because it was funny, but at the same time it wasn't, and my laughter turned to tears. I tried to hide it, but there was no hiding anything with Ms. Bartlett. "Oh, Kit, just let it out," she said as she held me while I cried.

After a few minutes, I tried to pull myself together. "Come on," I said. "Let's get this mess cleaned up."

"I'll do it," she said.

I wiped the tears from my face. "It's okay. I made the mess; I'll clean it up."

"We'll do it together," she said.

She started on the spill and I started on the glass.

"He's certainly a piece of work," she said, mopping up the puddle of booze.

"That's an understatement."

"Your mother…will she ever…?"

"Nope. She's dedicated to the man. God knows why."

Ms. Bartlett shook her head.

"Don't worry," I said. "I can handle him."

"Yes, Kit, but you shouldn't have to."

I smiled. "That's what Iggy said."

"It's not right," she said. "You shouldn't have to put up with it."

"Is that why you said I could stay with you instead of moving to St. John's?"

"They told you about that?"

I dumped a dustpan full of glass into a plastic bag. "Kind of. Dad blurted it out. During a drunken fit."

"It was just a suggestion. But they wouldn't go for it. I just thought it would do you some good. To live somewhere quiet for a while."

"Without him."

"Yes," she said. "Without him."

"I would have said yes, you know."

"It would have been nice," she said.

"Yeah, but then again, maybe the way it turned out was best. I mean, if I was living with you, maybe you wouldn't have found romance and got married."

Ms. Bartlett laughs. "True."

"Are you happy?"

"Yes, Kit. Very happy. Frank is a wonderful man."

"I was surprised when I heard. It's funny how things turn out sometimes."

"Yes," said Ms. Bartlett. "You never know what life will bring. Things can turn on a dime. And if there's one thing we never run out of, it's hope."

Maybe there was hope for my pathetic life yet.

I STOOD IN front of the mirror, looking like the poster child for the Hideously Ugly Pathetic Loser Society. It was my first day back at my old school, and I was pretty sure wearing high-waisted jeans from Bartlett's and a T-shirt with a faded Care Bear decal would not qualify as "going all out." But I'd been so busy taking care of Nan, the last thing on my mind was laundry, and all my good clothes—the ones Mom had bought me—were either dirty or wrinkled.

I opened a tube of lipstick I'd found in Nan's medicine cabinet. I wondered what Anne-Marie would think of "old lady red." I put some on and puckered at my reflection. It looked awful. I threw the lipstick in the garbage and called Elliot.

He answered after two rings.

"Hello?"

I could tell by his voice that I had woken him.

"Tell me I'm gorgeous."

"Huh?"

"Tell me I'm gorgeous."

"No."

"What?"

"I said no."

"Why?"

"Because I don't need to say it out loud for it to be true."

I smiled.

"I hope you're smiling."

"I am."

"So, how's Parsons Bay?"

"People suck."

"I'll never let you down."

"I know." I looked at the clock. "I have to go."

"Yeah, me too. I better get up and get ready for school."

"Bye, Moptop."

"*Au revoir, ma petite souris.*"

"Um, okay. Bye."

I hung up the phone and went back to the mirror. I grabbed some tissues and wiped my lips clean. I wondered what *souris* meant. I looked at the clock again to see if I had time to look it up but then decided that it didn't really matter—it could have meant "troll" or "dragon" or "hideously pathetic loser," but Elliot would have meant it in the nicest possible way.

I MADE DAD promise to stay home and look after Nan while I was at school every day. He said he would, but I didn't trust him, so I asked Ms. Bartlett to check in as often as she could.

My first month back in Parsons Bay pretty much sucked. I dreaded going to school every morning. The kids I had once hung out with had become clones of each other. They dressed the same, wore their hair the same way and talked about the same things, and everything they talked about was stuff I had no clue about, stuff that had happened after I moved to St. John's. Everything seemed to be a big in-joke that I wasn't in on.

And I never thought I'd say it, but I dreaded going back to Nan's at the end of the day too. There was no bread and molasses waiting for me, only a useless lug of a father giving me grief and my poor sick Nan, hidden under a pile of blankets, giving me weak smiles. My strong, sturdy Nan now a wilting flower.

I missed my St. John's life. I missed my mom and Iggy and Mr. Adams and Caroline. But most of all I missed Elliot.

IT FELT LIKE someone was punching through the skin of my chest with two hands and wrenching my heart every time I heard Nan cough. Nighttime was the worst. When Nan was coughing, I'd toss and turn; when she wasn't, I'd shiver outside her door, my ear pressed hard against it, listening for her soft snores.

And on the morning of February 14, when I saw the bloodstained tissues in the garbage, it was like whoever had grabbed my heart had decided to rip it into a million little pieces. I'd never imagined that on my first Valentine's Day with a boyfriend, my heart would be broken.

When I told Dad about the blood, his face went all sober-looking. That's when I knew it was bad. An ambulance came to take her to the hospital.

"We'll take good care of her," the paramedic said, but I couldn't shake the bad feeling that washed over me as they wheeled my beautiful, sweet Nan out of her little blue house, loaded her into the ambulance and took her away.

I called Elliot in tears.

"Can you hear this?" he said.

"What?"

"This."

"That scratchy sound?"

"Yeah. It's a zipper. I'm packing my bag. See you soon."

SEVEN

Two Fights, Both Lost

My nails were almost bitten off by the time his bus pulled into the station. It was almost eleven at night, dark and cold.

I watched the passengers get off.

Slowly.

How many people can you fit on a bus anyway?

The windows were dark.

I could see shadows.

But not his.

Did he sit in the very back seat or what? Why would he sit in the very back seat?

A punch in the gut. Maybe he had changed his mind.

I smacked him when I saw him. "Did you sit in the very back seat or what?"

"That's where the cool people sit."

"I almost had a heart attack."

"Come here and give me a hug."

"I didn't tell my dad you were coming. I didn't get a chance."

"It'll be fine. Me and your dad are cool."

WHEN WE WALKED through the door, Dad jumped up from his chair and gave Elliot a huge hug.

"I've missed you!" he said. "It's been too long. Too too too too long."

Elliot and I looked at each other. Dad reeked of booze.

I told Dad that Elliot would be staying a couple of nights.

He clapped his hands together and yelled, "Splendid!" He tore the cushions off the couch and yanked the sofa bed out. "*Voila!*" He stared at the bare mattress and then stuck his finger in the air. "Be right back!"

When he left the room, Elliot pulled me close for a hug. "This is the weirdest Valentine's Day ever."

"I'm just glad you're here," I said.

"Your nan will be okay, Kit."

I wrapped my arms tighter around his waist, no longer feeling alone.

Dad came back with a sheet and a blanket. He tried to tuck the sheet in and fell onto the bed. He couldn't get back up again. He was flipping around like a fish on dry land.

"Geez, Dad," I said. "You're as useless as a one-legged man in an arse-kicking competition."

Elliot swallowed a laugh. We watched my father try to make the bed for about ten minutes. At one point Elliot stepped forward to help, but I put out my arm and stopped him. When the bed was finally made, Dad said in a happy-go-lucky voice, "Well, whaddyathink?"

I mimicked his happy-go-lucky voice perfectly. "I think you're drunk!"

Elliot elbowed me in the ribs. "It looks great, Mr. Ryan."

I kept in character. "I agree, Mr. Ryan! It's swell. I mean, get a load of those corners! Why, you're a regular little Susie Homemaker. Somebody give this man a medal!"

"Are you being smart with me, young lady?"

Elliot stepped between us and patted the mattress. "Nice and firm. I'll have a great sleep tonight."

My father smiled. "Make yourself at home, young man."

Elliot took my dad's hand and shook it. "Thank you, sir, I really appreciate it. I'll only be here two nights. Back to school on Wednesday."

"Please," slurred Dad. "Call me Phonse."

I stared at them in amazement. They were like best buds.

Dad opened the fridge. "Wanna beer, Edward?"

"He's underage. And his name's Elliot."

Elliot plugged in the kettle. "Sit your bums down and I'll make some tea. How about a game of cards, Phonse?"

Dad beamed. "Sure!"

My boyfriend sure had a way with drunken losers.

We played 120s, Rummy 500, and Crazy Eights. Elliot and Dad bounced jokes and witty remarks off each other all night long. They were having a great time. And it pissed me off.

THE NEXT MORNING over breakfast, I asked Elliot how he could like my dad so much, after all I'd told him.

"It's not so much that I *like* him. I tolerate him, that's all. It's better than fighting."

"Suggesting a game of cards is more than tolerating," I said, scraping butter across my toast louder and faster than I needed to.

"It's called making the best of a bad situation. I figured a game of cards would keep him busy. Better than watching him sitting in that ugly recliner getting plastered."

Elliot poured milk into his cereal. He was using my old Kellogg's Corn Flakes bowl.

"Hey, that's my mine," I said.

"What?"

"My bowl. Nan got it for me when I was little. I always used it when I visited."

"Oh, do you want it back or something?"

"No, I'm just saying."

He took a big spoonful of Cheerios.

"His name is Corny, you know," I said.

Elliot looked around. "Who?"

"The rooster. In the bottom of the bowl."

"Really?"

"Yeah."

He swirled the contents of the bowl so he could catch a glimpse of the bottom. "I never knew that."

"I didn't either. Until I got the bowl. It's short for Cornelius or something."

"Cool."

I picked the crust off my toast. "So do you actually like him or what?"

"Who? The rooster? Nah, I prefer Tony the Tiger."

"Ha, ha, very funny," I said. "I meant my dad."

Elliot picked the crusts off my plate and ate them. "Of course not. He's an asshole."

"So you don't like him."

"*Je ne l'aime pas.*"

"Wow. Then that was an amazing performance last night. You deserve an Academy Award."

Elliot put his tea down. "Look, your father is probably never going to change. So you need to find a way to deal with him. I'm not saying fake it and be his best friend, but if you show a little interest in him every now and then, he might be a bit more tolerable. Did you see his face light up when I asked him to play cards? He was in a good mood the rest of the night. He wasn't so lonely."

"Lonely? My dad's not lonely. He has a family. He has drinking buddies. He's not alone."

Elliot picked up his cereal bowl and drank the last bit of milk. "Yeah, he has a family—a family who hates him. No wonder he freaks out all the time."

I slammed my mug down on the table. "He deserves it. Why are you defending him?"

"I'm not. I just—"

I started clearing the breakfast table. Noisily.

"I'm just giving you another point of view."

"Well, you can stick that point of view where the sun don't shine, because it sucks."

I threw the dishes into the sink of water and started washing them. Elliot came up behind me and put his arms around my waist. He whispered in my ear.

"I don't want to fight with you. I'm just saying, I dunno, maybe you should try not to push his buttons so much."

I spun around. "Try not to push his buttons? Are you friggin' kidding me?"

Elliot leaned against the counter and folded his arms. "*Regular little Susie Homemaker*? Come on, Kit. You know those snarky comments are going to piss him off."

I threw a handful of cutlery in the dish drainer. "You have no idea what it's like."

"No, I don't. But remember that quote about being a prisoner? Seriously, Kit, being mad all the time is bad for you. You're going to explode someday."

"I'm going to explode right now if you don't stop making excuses for my asshole father."

"Look, I admit I don't know what it's like, but he seems pretty harmless and—"

I gripped the edge of the sink and stared into the dirty dishwater. "Harmless?"

"So he gets a bit obnoxious when he drinks. I mean, you can deal with that, right?"

I took a couple of deep breaths to avoid saying something I'd regret.

"Kit?"

"You just don't get it, do you?" My voice was angry, hard.

"Then tell me. What's it like? Talk to me."

I looked out the kitchen window. "He hit my mom once. Right in the face."

Elliot paused. "Oh."

"And he's come close to hitting me a million times. If flinching were an Olympic sport, I'd probably get gold."

Elliot reached for my hand. I pulled away.

"But then again, if he gave me a good smack I'd probably deserve it, right? Because of my snarky comments? Because I pushed his buttons?"

"I'm sorry, Kit."

"I spend my whole life walking on eggshells because I never know if he's happy or mad or sad or if I'm going to say the wrong thing. My whole life, Elliot. As long as I can remember. The shouting, the swearing, the smell... you really have no idea. None."

I dried my hands and wiped my eyes with a dishtowel.

Elliot reached for my hand again. I let him take it. "I'm such an arsehole."

"Yeah. You are."

"I just...I dunno, I've never known an alcoholic before— not that that's an excuse or anything. I just thought he was a pain in the butt...I didn't know how bad things really were."

"Well, you do now."

Elliot put his arms around me and pulled me in tight. Things got quiet, each of us lost in our own thoughts.

"I don't know what to do now," he said finally.

I looked up. "What do you mean?"

"Well, I can't go back to St. John's now, can I? I can't leave you here, alone, with him."

"You have to go back. You can't stay here. What about school? You're already missing two days."

"Then why don't you leave? Move back with Iggy?"

"Because Nan needs me."

Elliot sighed.

"Don't worry. I can handle myself."

"But what if he—"

"I have to be here for Nan, and that's that."

He put his chin on the top of my head. "I'm sorry, Kit."

"I know."

"I love you."

"I love you too."

Elliot kissed the tip of my nose. "Sit your bum down. I'll finish these dishes. Then we'll go see your nan."

I sat at the table and watched Elliot make a mess of cleaning up. Water sloshed out of the sink and ran down the cabinets to the floor. The draining rack was full, but he kept stacking it with sudsy dishes, one on top of the other like a crazy game of Jenga.

"She's not the same," I said.

"Who?"

"Nan. She's all small and sick-looking. It makes me really sad."

Elliot turned around. "They'll take good care of her, Kit."

"I know. I just feel guilty because, well, I didn't go to the hospital yesterday after the ambulance took her. I panicked and called you instead."

"It's okay to be scared."

"But she could have died."

"But she didn't. You're going to see her today. That's all that matters now, right?"

I nodded, but I guess I didn't look convinced, because Elliot dried his hands and came to the table.

"What's wrong, Kit?"

"I'm nervous about the whole hospital thing. What if she looks even worse? What if she's hooked up to stuff?"

"Kit, she's sick. She'll probably look like shit. And, yeah, she'll probably be hooked up to stuff. But I bet it'll do her a world of good to see you. So once I finish these dishes, we're going to get ready and we're going to the hospital. You and me. Together. Okay?"

I nodded and blinked back some tears. "Moptop?"

"Yeah?"

"You're simply perfect."

He put his head down and shook it. "Aw, shucks. *Je suis embarrassé.*"

"Okay, dork, enough of that," I said, pulling myself together. "You look stupid. Like that bashful dwarf from Snow White."

He grabbed me by my waist and threw me over his shoulder, hanging my head over the sink full of dirty dishwater. "No one calls me a dwarf! Take it back!"

"Never!"

He put me down and we kissed until we heard the creaking of Dad getting out of bed upstairs.

NAN DID LOOK like shit, but she was awake and able to talk. She adored Elliot. He sat by her bedside and listened patiently as she told stories through an oxygen mask. Her voice was breathy and muffled, as if she were channeling Darth Vader, but Elliot leaned in close and hung on every word. He asked her what it was like growing up in Parsons Bay, and in a faint, halting voice she told him how plentiful the fish were all those years ago and how they were happier, simpler times. "What was Kit's dad like as a kid?" he asked. It was something I'd never bothered to ask.

She looked a bit distant for a minute—sad, almost—then said, "He was a little rascal, rambunctious and rowdy."

"And now he's a big rascal, rambunctious and rowdy," I said.

She gave a strained and sleepy laugh. "Excuse me while I rest my eyes a bit."

After she fell asleep, I took Elliot up to the top of the cliff. He sat on a boulder and I sat on his lap. It was cold right down to the bone, but we stayed there for ages, looking at the humongous ocean and listening to its waves, rambunctious and rowdy.

WE PASSED ANNE-MARIE on the way down. Toby was pulling her up the hill. Her face was red from trying to hike in a pair of ridiculously high heels. "Hey, girlfriend!" she shrieked. She held my shoulders and kissed the air on either side of my face.

Elliot looked at me as if to say, "Who the heck is that?" and I felt embarrassed. For me and for Anne-Marie.

"A bunch of us are hanging out at Will Hanrahan's tonight," she said. "Wanna come?"

"Yeah, maybe."

"Laters."

We watched as Toby pushed Anne-Marie up the trail by her butt cheeks.

Elliot shook his head. "I'm glad you're not that high-maintenance."

"She used to build sheds and install toilets."

"What? No way!"

"It's true. Total tomboy."

When we got down to the cove, I pointed at a fishing boat. "That used to be the *Kitty Charmer*."

"Really?"

We went onto the wharf for a closer look.

"Look," Elliot said. "It's got a new name: *Breakin'
Wind.*"

We broke down laughing. When we recovered,
I reached out and touched the faded blue shadow that hid
beneath the new red letters.

"Can you see it, Moptop?"

He put his hand over mine.

"Yeah, I see it. Does it make you sad?"

"Kind of. My dad used to keep these words freshly
painted. They were a beautiful sky-blue."

"Did he take you out on it much?"

"Once. We shared a Kit Kat."

"Do you wish your family still owned it?"

I thought about it for a minute. "No."

"How come?"

"Because if we still owned it, that would mean Dad still
had a job and we wouldn't have had to move to St. John's."

Elliot smiled. "And?"

I smirked. "And then I would never have met
Mr. Adams."

"And?"

"And Caroline."

He grabbed me around the waist and twirled me out
and over the water. "How would you like to be thrown
into the bay?"

"Okay, okay," I shrieked. "And then I never would have met you!"

He stopped spinning me and put me back down on the wharf. "And?"

"And that would be bad?"

"Yes, it would," he said, pulling me against him. "Very bad."

He wrapped his fingers around the belt loops of my jeans and pulled me toward him. I wondered if he tingled like I did. He leaned in for a kiss, but I stopped him. "Hang on a sec." I looked around the cove and then clambered over the side of the boat. I tried the door to the cabin. It was open. I signaled for Elliot to follow. He did. Like a lovesick puppy.

We went straight to the bottom bunk, giggling and whispering at first, but then Elliot slid his hand inside my shirt and laid it on my stomach and I kind of stopped breathing. I think he did too. I think he was scared to rest his hand there—it was halfway between hovering and landing. A few seconds later, though, it relaxed, sort of like butter on a warm pancake—at first it just sits there, cold and rigid, but then it melts over the surface. My tummy probably felt a bit pancake-ish too, all soft and doughy. At first I thought, *Oh shit, I really should work out more,* but then I thought, *Who cares? I bet Elliot doesn't.* With the full weight of his hand finally on my belly, he rolled to his side and put his head on my shoulder, and we talked for a bit. The light was fading outside and the boat was getting chilly, so I pulled the comforter up over us, and with the rocking of the boat we got kind of dozy, and it was in this sleepy, dopey state that we allowed our hands to roam. But the problem with things that feel good is they leave you wanting more and more. Like the feel of Elliot's shoulder muscles underneath his shirt. The taste of his lips. The touch of his fingers as his hand moved just underneath the waistband of my jeans. I didn't pull away. I just gave him another kiss and said, "We should go, Moptop" and he said, "Okay" and gave me a cuddle that led to a kiss that led to a touch. I could have stayed in that bunk forever. "Seriously," I said. "We should go." So he kissed my forehead and helped me up. We sneaked off the boat, stifling our giggles, and ran away from the cove.

Outside Cathy's Café and Corner Shop, Elliot felt in his pocket. "Wait here."

He went inside and came back with a Kit Kat. As soon as I saw it, my eyes filled with tears.

He put his arm around me. "Oh, Kit. It's just a Kit Kat."

But it was more than that.

"Don't mind me," I said, breaking it in half. "I'm just being a huge dork."

"Nah," he said. "Chocolate is a very emotional thing. You should see me Easter morning. As soon as I set eyes on those solid bunnies and foil-wrapped eggs, I bawl my eyes out."

I smacked him on the bum.

"Easy, tiger," he said. "We're off the boat now. Time to act respectable."

I laughed. "I wish you didn't have to go tomorrow."

"Me too. Coming for two nights was kinda pointless. I mean, your nan's still in the hospital. I haven't done much to help."

"What do you mean?" I said. "You have been a *great* help. I was freaking out and you came right away. Just being around you makes me feel, I dunno, calm."

Elliot closed his eyes and pretended to meditate, his hands held out in front of him, thumb and forefinger joined. "I am the king of Zen. Om."

I slapped him on the arm. "King of dorks, you mean."

He opened his eyes. "You have just broken my deep state of thoughtless awareness."

"I'll break something if you don't stop being a freak. Come on, let's go back to Nan's."

We walked toward home, sharing the Kit Kat. On the way, I showed him my school. We went behind it where nobody could see us and shared a chocolatey kiss.

IT WAS ELLIOT who suggested we go to Will Hanrahan's.

"Why not? We don't have anything else to do."

"We could play cards with my dad."

"Very funny."

"What if it's lame?"

"If it's lame we'll leave."

"Promise?"

"Promise. We'll even have a code word."

"A code word?"

"Yeah, like…banana."

"Banana?"

"Yeah, banana. Say you're in deep conversation with Anne-Marie about world peace…"

"And you call *me* sarcastic?"

"Okay, say you're in deep conservation with Anne-Marie about hiking in high heels…"

I laughed. "Continue."

"Then I would interrupt and say something like, 'Kit, did you know that eating a banana before a hike gives you lots of energy?' and that would be your cue to wrap things up so we could leave."

"That's totally dumb. You can't fit a word like banana into any old conversation."

"Try me."

"Okay, say I'm talking to Anne-Marie about what an idiot my dad is."

"Then I'd laugh and say, 'Your dad…he's such a silly ol' banana.'"

"Then I'd laugh and say, 'Moptop, you're such a dork.'"

"Then I'd laugh and say, 'But you love me anyway.'"

"And then I'd laugh and say, 'Yeah, I guess I do.'"

"And then we'd both laugh and start making out right there in front of everyone."

I smacked him. "Easy, tiger."

"So, we'll go?"

"All right, we'll go."

GETTING DOWN INTO Will Hanrahan's rec room required balance, as the stairs were dotted with clumps of kids smoking and drinking. This was clearly a full-blown party…and on a Monday night too.

I grabbed Elliot's hand tightly. "You won't drink, will you?"

"Not after last time. My guts are still sore from puking."

The room smelled musty and yeasty, like old books and spilled beer.

Anne-Marie was huddled with a group of girls. "Hey, girlfriend!" she yelled, pulling me into her circle and leaving Elliot standing awkwardly on his own.

"Love his hair," whispered a girl with raccoon-inspired eye makeup.

They all turned and stared at him. Elliot looked behind him to see what they were looking at, and when he realized it was him, he gave a dorky wave.

Anne-Marie laughed. "He's such a geek."

I shot her a dirty look.

"In a good way," she added.

A busty girl wearing a crop top spoke up. "What's his name?"

I *so* didn't want to be there. "Elliot."

"Tell her what you call him though," urged Anne-Marie.

I let out a bored sigh. "Moptop."

This set them off cackling like a bunch of witches.

"What's he like?" asked a girl who smelled like my father's chair.

I had to get out of there. "He's great."

"No, I mean, what's he *like*? You know, in the bedroom department?"

More witchlike cackles.

"I gotta go get a…beer." I backed away from the group and grabbed Elliot's arm, pulling him toward the stairs.

He laughed. "Is there a cauldron in the middle of that circle?"

"I know. It's like Halloween over there."

"I take it you'd like to leave?"

"Yep. Five minutes in and I'm done."

"You were right. We would've had more fun playing cards with your dad. Let's go."

We were going up the stairs when Elliot grabbed the back of his head.

"Aw, shit!" he yelled.

"What's wrong? What is it?"

He didn't answer but just kept holding the back of his head, a dazed look on his face.

I looked around the room, trying to make sense of what had happened. A beer bottle lay at Elliot's feet. Toby Burt and Will Hanrahan stood in the corner, laughing.

The room fell silent.

I stormed over to Toby and Will. "Why the hell did you do that?"

"Do what?" Toby shrugged.

"I know it was one of you assholes."

Anne-Marie rushed over and stood between us. "Back off, Kit. It wasn't Toby."

"How do you know?"

"I just know."

"Well, one of them did it."

Anne-Marie put her face close to mine. "You shouldn't go throwing accusations around."

"Your stupid boyfriend shouldn't go throwing beer bottles around."

"Come on, Kit," Elliot called. "Let's just go."

"Hey, Afro boy!" said Will. "You just going to run away and let you girlfriend fight your battles?"

"What battle? I don't even know you jerks."

"Call us jerks again and you'll know exactly what battle."

I pushed Anne-Marie out of my way, stood on my tiptoes and screamed in their faces, "Jerks!"

Toby Burt grabbed me by the shoulders and pushed me backward so hard that I fell to the floor, bonking my head as I landed.

The room was spinning. "Nice boyfriend," I said to a blurry Anne-Marie.

Someone came up behind me and slid his hands under my arms, pulling me to standing, and I didn't have to turn around to see it was Elliot. I knew his touch and I knew his smell. He set me on the couch and whispered, "Don't move an inch. Stay here, out of the way." Then, calmly and purposefully, he walked up to a smirking Toby Burt, who laughed and said, "What are you gonna do, Little Orphan Annie?"

"This," said Elliot. He punched Toby quickly and accurately, square in the face.

Toby fell to the floor, his face in his hands. Will pounced on Elliot. He sat on his chest, grabbed his collar and screamed in his face, "You broke his nose, you lunatic. Now I'm going to break your face!"

Some kids screamed for them to stop. Others started chanting, "Fight!" And when Will punched Elliot once, then twice, one kid said they were calling the cops.

At first I sat on my hands so I wouldn't move, but on the third punch I jumped up and yelled for someone, *anyone*, to get Will off him. The person who finally did was Toby.

He yanked on Will's shirt. "Will! Stop! Get off him! Someone's going to call the cops!" Will got up and backed away. Elliot's face was puffy, his eyes were almost swollen shut, and blood trickled from his nose. I tried not to cry. I bent down and helped him up. "You look as bruised as an old banana."

He gave a pained laugh. "It's a bit too late for the code word."

I guided him up the stairs. As we walked out Will Hanrahan's front door, I thought I heard Anne-Marie call my name. But I didn't turn around. I didn't care if I ever saw her again.

Dad flipped out when he saw us. He ran to the bathroom and raided the medicine cabinet. He pulled out bottles and bandages and creams and practically threw them at me.

He was on the edge of hysteria. "Do something, Kit! Fix him!"

I picked up one of the tubes. "Hemorrhoid cream is not going to help, Dad."

He was pacing. "Ice, ice—that's what we need. Ice."

While he ran to the freezer, I ran to Ms. Bartlett's. Within minutes she was in the house and in control. She examined the back of Elliot's head and put a Baggie of ice on the huge lump that had formed. She cleaned the blood off his face and looked in his eyes, asking him if he knew what day it was and where he was.

Satisfied with his answers, she said, "He'll be okay."

Dad poured Elliot a small drop of something strong and put it in his hand.

"Get this down ya, son."

"Dad!" I protested, but Ms. Bartlett put her hand on my shoulder and whispered, "He's just trying to help." So I let it go.

When I explained what had happened, I started shaking and crying uncontrollably. It was like some kind of delayed reaction.

Dad freaked out. "That bastard pushed you, Kitty? Are you okay? Your head—does it hurt?"

"My head's fine, Dad," I said. "But I don't think Elliot's is."

Dad started pacing again. "Well, we should call the cops, right? I mean, this is assault and battery!"

Ms. Bartlett put the kettle on.

"There's no point," said Elliot. "I threw the first punch."

I blew my nose and wiped my eyes with a tissue. "But they threw a bottle at your head!"

"Yeah, but no one can prove that. Everyone there saw me punch that guy in the face. I shouldn't have reacted. I should have just left."

"You would have if it wasn't for me. This is all my fault. I shouldn't have screamed in their faces. I should have walked away."

Ms. Bartlett passed me a warm facecloth. "Calm down, love. Give your face a wash."

"You were right, Kit," said Elliot. "We should never have gone in the first place."

The creaking of the floorboards was driving me nuts. Ms. Bartlett took my dad by the arm and sat him in his chair.

"Shoulda, coulda, woulda," she said. "What's done is done. Elliot's right: there's no point in calling the police. Every kid in town is going to say he started it, and where will that leave him?"

Dad poured himself a big drink. "As usual, nice guys finish last. It's not bloody fair."

Ms. Bartlett put a pot of tea on the table. "No, it's not."

Elliot took a sip of Dad's drink and grimaced. Ms. Bartlett swapped it for a cup of tea and said she'd better get back to Frank.

"Wake him every hour tonight, Kit. We want to make sure he doesn't have a concussion. If you can't wake him, come get me right away."

When my alarm went off the first time that night, I went downstairs and saw Dad sitting in the kitchen with a pot of tea. "I already checked him," he said. "Go back to bed, love." And I was grateful, because I was awfully tired. I reset my alarm, and when I went down an hour later, Dad was still sitting there at the table. "Just checked him. He's fine. Go to bed, love. No need to set your alarm again. I got this."

I crawled back into bed and held my alarm clock in my hand. Elliot *had* to be woken every single hour. What if Dad passed out and forgot? I reset the alarm and put the clock on my bedside table. I closed my eyes. He was drinking tea, just tea. He had said, *I got this.* I reached out into the darkness of my bedroom, flipped the alarm off and didn't wake up again until morning.

ELLIOT LOOKED LIKE crap when he boarded the bus back to St. John's. I was worried his parents would take one look at him and never let him come to Parsons Bay again, but he said not to worry, that he could handle his parents.

I asked him to check on Mr. Adams for me and see how he was doing. A week later I got a letter in the mail.

Dear Kit,

I had a visit from your fancy man today, the one with the ginormous bird's nest on top of his head. His face was a mess. When I asked him what happened he stood on my door-step rambling on about how he had been to Parsons Bay and there was a party and you didn't want to go, but he did, and there was a fight and he got hit in the head. He went on and on and on for so long that I had no choice but to invite him in. I said, "Listen here, lad, I have no idea what you are on about, but I sense there's been trouble. Come in and we'll talk over tea." So we went into the kitchen and before he filled me in on the fracas at the party, he said, and I quote, "Sit your bum down, Mr. Adams. I'll get the tea." At first I thought, How rude! The impertinence! The impudence! The rudeness! The gall! But once I sat my bum down I thought, Lovely jubbly, how absolutely wonderful it is to be tended on. Speaking of which, I don't recall you ever telling me to sit my bum down. You, young lady, could take a page or two from Bird's Nest's book.

Anyhoo, he told me you were wondering how I was doing. Well, nosey parker, if you must know, I am fine.

I do miss our visits though.

And about that spot of bother you had at that party... mind yourself and keep your nose clean. If you dance with the devil you'll get poked by his horns.

May the force be with you,
Mr. Adams

I read the letter to Nan. She smiled and said she liked Mr. Adams's style.

"You'll meet him someday," I said.

"No, Kit, I won't."

"Don't say that."

"I love you, Kit," she said, and my heart was bursting and sinking at the same time.

"I love you too," I said. "See you next time."

But when I went to visit her the next day, her breathing was real bad and she was being moved to Intensive Care. I got scared and ran home, and when I told Dad, he looked scared too. We went back to the hospital together, where they told us that Nan was hooked up to a machine to help her breathe. "It doesn't look good," her doctor said. I felt like I might throw up. When I looked at Dad, the color had drained out of his face. It was hard to look at Nan with that horrible tube coming out of her mouth, but she was looking at me with glazed eyes. I didn't want her to know I was scared, so I faked a smile. Dad kept talking to her, telling her useless stuff like what kind of wonderful prizes there were on *The Price is Right* that morning. When the nurses said it was time for us to leave, I held Nan's hand. I tried not to cry, because that would just make her feel bad and dying was probably bad enough without feeling guilty about it.

When I went back the day after that, the nurses said they were sorry, and I said, "For what?" and then I realized she was gone. In movies when people are told that someone they love has died, their knees buckle and they collapse to the floor, screaming and bawling. But I was frozen. It was like my feet were stuck in mud. But the weirdest thing of all was how badly I wanted my dad. When I was finally able to speak, I asked the nurses about him. They said he had been there earlier and that he'd freaked out. They'd tried to talk to him, relax him, and asked him if he'd like to talk to the chaplain, but he'd taken off. *Like a shot*, they said.

He wasn't in the pub or the liquor store or his chair at home. Where was he? I needed him. I wondered if he, too, liked it at the top of the cliff, no matter what the weather, so I pulled up my hood and ran to the trailhead, fighting the wind and the rain the whole way. I was about to head up the hill when I saw, out of the corner of my eye, something lying on the wharf, right next to the *Breakin' Wind*. As I got closer I saw that it was Dad, passed out in the fetal position, an empty bottle and a puddle of vomit next to his face.

I grabbed his shoulders and shook him. "Dad! Wake up! Come on! Wake up!" The wind howled around us and the wharf bobbed like crazy, the stupid empty bottle rolling back and forth, back and forth, across the wooden planks. I tried not to look at his puke. I tried not to breathe in his stink. I hit him on the arm. "Dad! Will you just get up?" The bottle rolled this way. The bottle rolled that way. I hit him again. Harder. "I don't need this right now. Get up, you useless piece of shit!" I made a tight fist. I punched him. "Please. Get the hell up!" Rattle to the left. Rattle to the right. I let out a scream and snatched the bottle. I leaned off and threw it with all my might against the boat. It made a loud smash that woke my dad with a start. He looked confused. A tiny bit of me felt sorry for him. I closed my eyes and willed the anger out of my body so that it wouldn't show in my voice. "Get up, Dad. Let's go home. It's cold."

I thought about grabbing his hand and helping him to his feet, but I didn't. Instead, I left the big clump of disgusting, pathetic sadness on the wharf. But I walked home slowly enough for him to catch up.

NAN HAD BEEN dead for hours. And I hadn't shed a single tear. Not even when I returned to her empty house and was hit with the realization that she'd never set foot in it again.

"Get out of those wet clothes," I said to my father. "I'll make a pot of tea."

"I don't want tea," my father said. "I want something else."

I practically threw the kettle on the stove. "You're having tea."

He didn't argue.

I sat in Nan's rocker. I listened for the kettle's familiar whistle and stared at the familiar yellow walls. The house looked the same as ever, but it couldn't have felt more different. My eyes moved from the walls to the counter, where the biscuit tin sat empty. I was struck with the thought that I would never taste Nan's tea buns again. Yet deep inside I felt nothing. I was numb.

I rocked to the slow tick of the clock. One second felt like ten. Time dragged. And except for the creaking of Dad moving around on the floor above, the house was eerily silent. So when the kettle whistled, I didn't rush to take it off the heat. I allowed its piercing scream to fill the room. I left it to splutter and screech and rumble. I closed my eyes and rocked harder and faster. Noise is what I wanted. Crazy, meaningless noise.

Then it stopped.

"What the hell are you doing?" my father asked.

I opened my eyes. "Waiting for the kettle to boil."

"Kitty, love…"

I stood up. "I'll get the tea."

"No," he said. "I'll do it…if you want."

"I don't."

I poured the water into the pot and covered it with the multicolored tea cozy. I thought about Mr. Adams, who was the same age as Nan, and wished time would stand still.

My dad was hovering. "If you need to talk…"

I turned around. "About what?" I snapped.

His eyes filled with tears.

"We're out of sugar," I said. "I'll be back soon."

I bolted. Up to the cliff. Where I screamed and screeched louder and longer than any kettle ever could. Then I sat on a boulder and stared out at the ocean, struck by its unusual calm. The lashing rain and howling wind had stopped. Just like that. The weather was as unpredictable as my life.

EIGHT
The Funeral

Dad struck the match with a quick flick of his wrist. The smell of sulphur shot up my nose, tickling the hairs in my nostrils and making my eyes water.

"Geez, Dad, watch it. You're gonna set my hair on fire."

He probably thought it was his big moment, me and him hugging like this. It'd had the potential, I suppose, before he decided to light up a smoke in the middle of it.

The flame was at my eye level, and I watched it bring life to Dad's cigarette. A few quick puffs, and the end ignited—bright red turned orange and then black, mottled and Halloweeny. The embers got bright every time he took a big puff and went dim every time he exhaled. Bright, dim, bright, dim. It was fascinating to watch. A long ash formed on the end of the cigarette.

The longer he smoked, the longer it got. I waited for it to fall, but it didn't. How was that possible? It looked so fragile. The mixture of colors was beautiful. Too bad something so pretty can kill you.

He rested his hand on my head. I didn't say, *Move your bloody hand, you idiot* 'cause it might've seemed harsh considering that his mother was lying dead in the church-yard behind us. So I just stood there, stiff as a board, my arms dangling at my side.

He'd cried earlier. It made me feel weird—like when you wake up late and realize you're supposed to be some-where and everything feels wrong and it takes you ages to recover. His bottom lip trembled and I thought, *Oh shit, don't cry, please don't cry,* but he did and snot ran down his upper lip, and I had that waking-up-late feeling and was grossed out at the same time.

The smoke floating out of his mouth snaked up my nose and slithered down my throat and into my lungs, constricting them. I swallowed a cough and wondered why I was being so nice. He patted my back like I was a golden retriever. A crazy kind of patting that verged on whacking. He was *so* out of his comfort zone.

He made a big snuffling sound. I snuck a peek at him, hoping to God he wasn't crying again. His bloodshot eyes popped out from his pale face. He looked lost.

Maybe it was time to stop punishing him.

I sent a message to my brain, asking it to signal my arms to move from their rag-doll position and wrap around the little boy in my father's body. But either my brain ignored me or my arms ignored my brain; my arms weighed six million tons, and there was no way I was moving them.

I tilted my head and let it rest on his chest. Nothing happened. The world didn't come crashing down around me. Maybe I could do this.

I listened to the rattle in his chest. Didn't he know that smoking kills?

I suddenly thought about how stupid I must look. Standing in the middle of the church parking lot, my dad hugging me and me standing like a plank of wood.

"I'm glad you're here, Kitty."

His voice sounded like the boys at school—all croaky and weird.

"Don't know how I would have gotten through that service without you."

Don't be a dumbass, Kit. Hug the man.

It was like bungee jumping. I held my breath. Five, four, three, two, one, JUMP.

I wrapped my arms around his waist.

And held it.

I opened my eyes.

I'd made it.

I'd hugged him.

I'd hugged my father.

And I didn't feel queasy.

I actually felt okay.

I wanted to say something. Something nice. Not quite *I love you* or anything—I'd never say that—but something.

He spoke first.

"I could murder a whiskey right about now."

My arms dropped.

I noticed Iggy's car in the corner of the church parking lot and realized he'd been there the whole time, watching and waiting. He and Mom had arrived the day before, and I'd been thankful to not have to deal with my father alone. I stormed to Iggy's car and got in the front seat, slamming the door hard.

"He just said he could murder a drop of whiskey," I said, staring at my dad, who I'd left standing out in the cold. "I was trying to be all nice and supportive and then he goes and says that. It's like it's all he cares about."

"Well, at least he had the decency to wait until after the funeral," said Iggy.

"Big whoop," I said. "Come on. Let's go."

"We can't just leave him standing there, Kit," said Iggy. "Go get him. Everyone is at the pub, and they'll wonder what happened to us."

"He has a car," I grumbled. "He can drive himself."

Iggy ignored me and rolled down his window. "Phonse," he called. "Come with us. I'll give you a ride."

The whole town was in the pub. People said things like "She lived a good, long life," as if that made it okay. But it didn't. It was far from okay.

Dad got sloshed. I made a mental note to add The Grieving Drunk to the top of the Drunk-O-Meter, a step above The Mad Drunk.

Mom followed Dad around the pub, doing damage control. She interrupted him when he spoke to people, talked loudly over top of him and apologized for him if he said something off-color.

I sat in the corner with a glass of fruit punch, trying not to be noticed. I watched Iggy accept condolences and hugs from Nan's elderly friends, but he kept looking around, all distracted. I knew he was looking for me, and I should probably have waved or something, but I didn't feel like it. I figured he'd spot me eventually, and sure enough, he did. He sat down right next to me with his own glass of fruit punch.

"Here's to your nan," he said, and we clinked glasses.

"I wish Elliot was here," I said.

"I know. He really did try to come. Your mother and I were going to pick him up and everything. But he called at the last minute and said his parents wouldn't let him. He was really upset. I could hear it in his voice."

"It's because of the fight at Will Hanrahan's. They probably think I'm bad news. I'll never see Nan again, and now I'll probably never see Elliot again either."

Iggy put his arm around me. "Go introduce yourself when you come back to St. John's with us tomorrow. The minute Elliot's folks meet you, they'll know what a wonderful girl you are."

"But I'm not going back."

"What? Why not?"

"Because I need to stay here and—"

"And what, Kit? I don't get it. There's nothing here for you now."

"Iggy, just let me explain. What I meant was—"

"You can't stay in Parsons Bay. St. John's is your home now."

"Yes, but—"

"But nothing! Your mom is in St. John's, I'm in St. John's, *Elliot* is in St. John's—"

"Iggy!" I exclaimed. "Take a chill pill! Will you stop interrupting and let me explain? What I meant was I'm not coming back *tomorrow*. I'm going to stay here for a bit to help Dad sort Nan's things and get her house ready for sale."

"Oh," said Iggy. "Okay. But can't your Dad handle all that stuff? You've been through so much."

I spun my glass around and around on my place mat. "The thing is, well, um, Dad can't really be left on his own. Especially now."

"He's not your responsibility, Kit. He should be taking care of you, not the other way around. You need a break. I'll talk to your Mom, see if she can stay instead."

"She's already been fired once because of Dad. She needs to get back to work."

"Maybe she can take a week off or something."

"I've already talked to her. She has one week of holidays left, and she was saving them for summer. She offered to take them now instead, but I said no. She works hard. I want her to have fun on her holidays. Not spend them here dealing with this crap."

Iggy kissed the top of my head. "You're my favorite niece, you know."

I elbowed him in the side. "I'm your *only* niece."

He laughed. "I could stay if you want. Instead of you."

"Thanks, but I kinda want to go through Nan's things. It might help, you know?"

He nodded. "I'm going to paint your room for when you come back. What color do you want it?"

"Yellow. Like the den. Like Nan's kitchen."

"Yellow it is."

There was a loud shriek of feedback from the pub's sound system. Dad had turned on the karaoke machine.

"This one's for me mudder!"

Queen's "Another One Bites The Dust" erupted from the speakers.

My mother looked horrified. But me and Iggy, we fell over laughing.

THE TOP SHELF in Nan's closet was covered in shoe boxes.

"Might as well start here," said Dad, lifting them down one by one and laying them on the bed.

I took off my shoes and sat cross-legged on Nan's quilt. The room smelled of peppermints and Oil of Olay. Dad sat next to me and took the lid off a box. Sitting on the top was a photo of him as a baby, propped on his mother's knee. He took one look at it and broke down. I reached over to the bedside table and grabbed some tissues.

"It's okay, Dad."

He wiped his eyes and tried to pull himself together. "I wasn't a good son."

"That doesn't matter now."

"Been a troublemaker my whole life."

I reached into the box and took out another photo. An action shot of Dad in a snowsuit, jumping in midair above a crumpled snowman. A smaller kid next to him was bawling. "I see what you mean."

I passed Dad the photo.

"Who is that kid anyway?" I asked.

He looked at the picture, then laid it facedown on the bed. "Just some kid."

I picked the photo back up. "He's more than just some kid. I can tell. Who is he?"

Dad got up and went to the window. "This week's been bad enough without…"

"Without what?"

He shook his head. "Without dredging all that stuff up."

"What stuff?"

He turned around.

"There's stuff you don't know, Kitty."

"There is?"

He nodded.

"Tell me. The stuff. I want to know."

He sat back down on the bed and pointed to the photo in my hand. "That's Tom."

"Tom who?"

"My brother Tom."

"What? You don't have a brother."

"I did."

My heart sank. I looked at the chubby face poking out of the circle of fur on his snowsuit hood. He looked like a little lion.

"How old was he…when he…?"

"Seven. Seven bloody years old."

"I'm sorry, Dad."

I wanted to know how but couldn't bring myself to ask.

"He was a pain in the arse, but I loved the hell out of him."

I reached into the box and pulled out photo after photo, mostly of Tom.

"Nan has loads of old photos up around the house. How come she never put out any of Tom? Why are they hidden in this box? How come no one ever mentions him? I don't get it."

Dad didn't say anything. I kept piling photos on his lap, photos of him and Tom tobogganing, camping, fishing—pictures that should've brought back happy memories. But Dad looked sad.

I picked up an old black-and-white of Dad and Tom down at the cove. Dad was sticking his tongue out and rolling his eyes to the back of his head. Tom was laughing.

"Look at your face, Dad," I said in an attempt to cheer him up. "You must have been a real joker."

He smiled weakly.

I picked up another of Tom as a baby. "Aw, that's cute. Look how you're holding him. You guys must have been really close."

He nodded.

"Did your father take these pictures? He's not in any of the photos."

Dad gasped. He literally gasped. I actually heard a quick intake of air. It made my heart skip a beat because I was afraid it was his heart or something. I reached out and grabbed his arm.

"Dad? Are you okay?"

"I'm…I'm fine." He stood up, and the photos that were on his lap scattered to the floor. He bent over to pick them up but couldn't get a grasp on any because his hands were shaking too much. I hopped off the bed to help.

"Did I say something wrong, Dad? I'm sorry."

Dad sat back down on the end of the bed and sighed. "No, Kitty. You didn't say anything wrong. Leave those. Come sit next to me."

I picked up a shot of Nan. A beautiful, young Nan.

"Leave them, Kitty."

Splodges of wet fell onto the photo. I was ruining it.

"Kitty."

I collapsed to the floor and cried.

"Kitty, it's okay."

"No. It's not okay." I sniffed. "You're sad about Nan and now I've gone and made you sadder by bringing up the past, and I'm sad too, and I can't take it anymore and I don't know what to do."

Dad reached for me. "Your old man's here, Kitty." He put his hands gently over mine. They were rough and cold, but they made me feel warm. How was that possible?

I got up and sat with him on the end of the bed. He put his arm around me, and I rested my head against his chest. As easy as that.

I wondered if Nan was watching.

After a bit, Dad spoke.

"Tom's death was hard, real hard. And no one ever talks about it because of the way he died."

"You don't have to talk about it if you don't want to, Dad. It's okay."

Dad took my hand. He looked me in the eye.

"My father was a bad man, Kitty."

Then I knew. I knew the "stuff" he was talking about. My heart almost pounded out of my chest.

"Tom was a little bugger. He was always winding my father up. I knew to steer clear. But Tom always pushed his luck. All it took was one big smack. Tom went flying, hit his head on the radiator and that was that."

Dad passed me a tissue. "I never told you before because, well, kids don't need to know about stuff like that.

Look at you now—you look frightened. An⸍
it. I don't want you to look frightened."

I knew it'd hurt, but if I didn't say it n⸍ ⸍⸍⸍⸍
would.

"But Dad, you've frightened me. Lots of times. When
you'd throw stuff. Or scream. Or swear." I looked down.
"Or like that time you hit Mom."

He looked away. "Like father, like son."

"Wouldn't you make sure that didn't happen, Dad?
After what happened to Tom?"

"The last thing I wanted to be was like him. But then I
started drinking, and it went downhill from there. Turned
out like the old bastard anyway." He looked me in the eye
again. "But I've never laid a finger on you, Kitty. And I
never will."

I thought of the phrase "cold comfort."

"Did your dad go to jail?"

"No. He took off. Never saw him again."

"Did you love him?"

"What?"

"Your dad? Did you love him?"

My father thought for a moment. "He was my father.
So yeah, I loved him. I loved him a lot. I just hated the
things he did."

"Remember when I said I hated you? After Caroline
came for dinner that time?"

His eyes filled with tears, and when he spoke his voice was tight and choked. "I'll never forget it."

"I don't, Dad. I don't hate you. I just hate the things you do."

He sniffed and nodded.

I reached out and touched his arm. "I actually…love you."

He couldn't talk for a bit, so I just left my hand on his arm. Eventually he spoke.

"I love you too."

THE NEXT MORNING I woke up shivering. My feet were like ice. Wind and rain rattled the house. I looked out the window but couldn't see a thing. It was like someone had a hose aimed right at the window.

I pulled on a hoodie and a warm pair of socks and went downstairs. I put a teabag in a cup, then changed my mind and put a couple in the pot instead, enough for me and Dad. I plugged the kettle in and waited. But the kettle didn't boil. I flicked the light switch. On, off, on, off. Nothing.

I knocked on Dad's door. "Dad? The power's out. Should we start a fire in the fireplace?"

No response.

"Dad?"

I went to my room and took my watch off the bedside table. Nine thirty. It wasn't too early. I decided to wake him.

I banged on his door. "Dad?" I peeked into the room. His bed was empty.

I got a funny feeling and went back downstairs. I checked the living room. His chair was empty. I picked up the phone, not knowing who I'd call. The line was dead anyway.

Where would he go in the middle of a storm?

I pulled on a coat and slipped into a pair of rubber boots. The wind almost took off the door. The hose was directed at me now. I ran to Ms. Bartlett's.

Ms. Bartlett had to shout to be heard above the gale. "Kit? What is it?"

"Is Dad here?"

"No. Why?"

"He's gone! He's not in his bed!"

"He'll turn up," she said. "Now come in before you freeze to death."

"I have to find him."

Ms. Bartlett yelled again, but this time she was mad. "You are not going anywhere! Come in this house right now!"

"I can't! I have to find him!"

I ran into the storm.

The pub wouldn't be open. Or the liquor store. And he had no friends.

I felt sick.

I went directly to the cove. It was gone. The *Breakin'*
Wind was gone.

IT WAS TOO dangerous for the search-and-rescue team. That's
what the RCMP guy said. He said that as soon as it was
safe, the coast guard would send out some boats and a
helicopter. He said he was sorry. He said he'd drive me
home. We couldn't see a thing through his windshield.
I watched the wipers struggling to swish back and forth.
Useless, like everything else.

He stopped the car in front of Nan's. "Is there someone
home?"

I shook my head.

"You shouldn't be alone."

I directed him to Ms. Bartlett's.

He came in and told Ms. Bartlett what had happened.
Fisty Hinks—Frank—was there, making things feel even
more surreal.

The Mountie said he'd keep us posted and left us alone
in the cold, dark house. Ms. Bartlett sat me down by the
fire. The power was still out, and the windows rattled.

"He's out there in this. By himself," I said. "He's probably
drunk. He probably doesn't have a clue what he's doing."

Frank put a towel around my shoulders. "It's amazing what people can manage in an emergency."

"What am I supposed to do now?"

He squeezed my shoulder. "Wait."

DOZENS OF PEOPLE braved the weather and packed themselves into Ms. Bartlett's house. They made tea on camping stoves and they prayed. Someone started singing "The Petty Harbour Bait Skiff," a folk song about a fishing boat that got caught in bad weather, leaving the whole crew drowned but one. Soon others joined in, and the room filled with song.

> *Good people all, both great and small, I hope you will attend,*
> *And listen to these verses few that I have lately penned.*
> *And I'll relate the hardships great that fishermen must stand*
> *While fighting for a livelihood on the coast of Newfoundland.*

The singing sounded good. They had the harmonies down pat. But the song choice sucked. They should have picked something more suited to the situation. I mean, they were singing about the bravery of young fishermen who risked their lives to earn a living while my dad was lost at sea out of stupidity—he didn't *need* to get on that boat. He was probably drunk and didn't know what he was doing—or maybe he was drunk and knew exactly what he was doing. Either way, there was nothing brave or valiant about it all.

Your heart would ache, all for their sake, if you were standing by,
To see them drowning, one by one, and no relief being nigh;
Struggling with the boisterous waves, all in their youth and bloom,
But at last they sank, to rise no more, all on the eighth of June.

Wow. These people were terrible cheerer-uppers. Shouldn't they be singing songs of hope? Or a song that reminded us of my dad? I imagined everyone bursting out into "Smoke! Smoke! Smoke! (That Cigarette)" and caught myself smiling. I hoped no one noticed.

By suppertime, the storm had eased. The RCMP officer arrived. They had started their search.

By bedtime, the electricity returned. There was still no sign of my father.

Ms. Bartlett made up a bed in the spare room. "Try to get some sleep."

The furnace hummed, but there was too much cold to heat. I could see my breath when I exhaled.

I was cold.

But Dad must be much, much colder.

Was he in the boat, lost?

Or had it sunk?

Was he floating in the Atlantic, dead?

Were his eyes open?

Was he scared?

He said he couldn't swim. He said it was just as well. Maybe he was right.

If he had drowned, I prayed that he was the drunkest he'd ever been in his whole life. I prayed he didn't feel a thing.

I KNEW THERE was no news, because it was late and no one had woken me.

I got up.

The house was warm now, and sun shone into the kitchen.

The RCMP guy sat at the kitchen table.

"They're still looking," he said. "But that storm was pretty severe."

I nodded.

He told me to sit down.

"The longer he's out there, the less chance he has of survival."

I nodded again.

"At some point, the search-and-rescue mission will turn into a recovery mission."

He got up to leave. "I'll be in touch as soon as I hear something."

Ms. Bartlett saw him out. Frank fixed me some breakfast. I watched as he made a pot of tea and buttered some toast.

"We used to call you Fisty, you know," I said. "Before you married Ms. Bartlett. When you lived alone."

"I know." He passed me my tea. "I was a miserable bugger back then."

"Remember Nan's seventieth birthday party?"

"I certainly do. You were quite the little dancer."

"It's one of my favorite memories ever," I said.

I was nine years old, and everyone from Parsons Bay had crammed themselves into Nan's little house. Anne-Marie and I were under the kitchen table. Jock Wilson was playing his fiddle and everyone was singing. When Frank walked in, Anne-Marie and I held hands real tight. *He'll murder us*, whispered Anne-Marie. *Then we better stay hidden*, I advised. No one else seemed to care that mean old Fisty Hinks was there at my nan's party. They just said, *Nice to see ya, Frank.* All Anne-Marie and I could do was sit and stare, but after a while we got bored and started playing clapping games. It was during "Mary Mack" that Fisty Hinks poked his head under the table and put his hand out to me. Anne-Marie and I jumped with fright, and I didn't know if I wanted to take that hand. After all, it was the same hand that was usually balled up in a fist. But up close, Fisty Hinks had a nice smile. So I took his hand. And we danced. I stood on his feet just like I saw other girls do with their fathers. Fisty told me I was a grand dancer and that his daughter used to dance on his feet too. That night I promised myself that I wouldn't run past his house anymore. But as soon as I was back out playing with my friends, I broke that promise. We'd run past his house, hearts beating with fear and excitement, screaming and yelling, waiting for him to come out and run us off, and when he did we'd take off laughing.

"I'm sorry we called you Fisty and tormented you. Kids can be so stupid sometimes."

"So can old men. I was a miserable old bastard."

"Mom said it was because you were sad."

"Your mother was right. I was very sad. And lonely."

"Why?"

"I lost my wife and daughter. In a car accident."

"I'm sorry. No one ever said."

"People find it hard to tell children these things."

Another dead child swept under the rug.

"It was a long, long time ago," he said.

"What was your daughter's name?"

"Catherine, with a *C*."

"Really? I'm Katherine too. With a *K*."

Frank smiled. "I know. It's such a lovely name."

"Dad started calling me Kitty for short. Sometimes I feel too old for it. Maybe I'll tell people to start calling me Katherine now."

"No matter what you call yourself, you'll always be Kitty to your father."

I burst out crying.

Poor Frank didn't know what to do, so he ran outside looking for Ms. Bartlett, and when he found her, she rushed in and held me until I was all out of tears.

MOM, IGGY AND Elliot arrived in the afternoon. Mom looked terrible. Iggy said she'd been beside herself since she heard the news.

"I came as soon as I could," she said. "They said the storm was bad and the roads were closed and—"

"It's okay, Mom."

Elliot hugged me. "I'm sorry about your nan. I'm sorry I missed the funeral. My parents, they wouldn't let me come and—"

I hugged him tight. "It's okay. You're here now."

"I told them I didn't care what they said, this time I was coming no matter what."

"I'm just glad you're here."

He gave me a card from Mr. Adams.

Dear Kit,

I heard your father is MIA *(missing in action). I sincerely hope he is found alive and well. But if he happens to pop his clogs, I will be here for you, in St. John's, with open arms and an overabundance of bickies. (I received a case full of digestives in the mail as a result of my complaint letter.)*

Sincerely,

Reginald Adams

Iggy gave me a strange look. "What's so funny?"

I passed him the card. He grinned and passed it to Mom.

"I suppose that's one way to put it." She managed a laugh. "But let's hope his clogs aren't popped yet. It's only day two. There's still hope."

Everyone nodded.

Except me.

We went back to Nan's.

And waited.

DAY THREE. RECOVERY mission.

They found the boat. Battered and empty. Mom bawled when they told her they were now looking for a body.

I grabbed my coat and ran.

Ten minutes to the top of the cliff.

A record.

The water was choppy.

Did he get smashed against a cliff?

Do whales eat dead bodies?

I closed my eyes. I pictured him floating gently on the waves, bobbing this way and that, smiling.

I squeezed my eyes, as if to make the image stick.

"I'm sorry, Kit."

I jumped. It was Anne-Marie.

"About your dad. And everything."

"It's okay."

She put her arm around me. "Are you going to stay in Parsons Bay?"

"No. St. John's is home now."

"Will you visit?"

I wanted to say, *Yes, to see Ms. Bartlett and Frank,* but that would have been mean, so I just said, "Yeah."

"Do you want to come back to my house for a cup of tea?"

"No, thanks. Elliot's here. I'm going to go hang out with him." I was tempted to add, *For some QT—you know, quality time?,* but now wasn't the time for spite.

"Oh, okay."

"Laters." I couldn't resist.

I walked down the trail and left Anne-Marie at the top, staring into the Atlantic. Elliot was at the bottom, waiting. He took my hand and we walked home.

THAT NIGHT WHILE everyone slept, I sat in the living room, staring at my father's empty recliner. Why he loved it so much was beyond me. Its orangey-brown plaid material was hideous. It was tattered and worn. And it smelled.

I imagined him in it. Passed out, sleeping it off, dead to the world, sloshed. I wanted to kick the hell out of that stupid chair. I hated it. And I hated him in it. I wanted to throw it over the side of the cliff so that they could be reunited, the stupid man and his stupid chair.

I stood up, walked over to it, ran my fingers across the arm. The material was rough and scratchy. I couldn't understand how he could even bear to sit in it. Then again, he was drunk most of the time and probably never noticed.

I sat on the arm and draped my upper half across the back. What a stupid chair. It was even uglier up close. Smellier too.

I imagined him in it. Sober this time. Me lounging above him, chatting to him. Father and daughter, having a laugh. Sliding my arm casually from the back cushion to his shoulder.

I slid into the seat. I'd never sat in his chair before, not even indirectly via his lap. Not that he hadn't tried. *Come here, Kitty. Come sit with your father.* But I could never stand to be that close, to smell his breath, to look into those red eyes, to listen to his gibberish.

I imagined he *was* the chair. He was the ugly fabric and the whiskey-soaked foam. He was the old wooden frame and the broken springs. I slipped my fingers into the rips that covered the arms, felt the spongy innards. Then I pulled. I clawed and I scratched and I tore, like a crazed cat with a scratching post. I cried and I bawled and I grieved. And I wished. I wished I was crying because I missed my father, not because I wished things had been different.

I loved him though.

And he loved me.

This was true.

And that was all that mattered now.

It had to be.

I curled up in a ball and slept, clutching a scrap of fabric from the stupid, ugly chair that was my father's.

THEY NEVER DID find his body. So we packed up and left. Elliot and I sat in the back of Iggy's car. I slept against him the whole way to St. John's.

MR. ADAMS SHOOK my hand, said, "My condolences" and put twenty-four digestive biscuits out for tea.

"He told me he loved me the day before he left," I said. "Everything was kind of okay between us for once. Why would he take off like that?"

"I don't know, flower. Maybe he knew he'd just go and disappoint you again."

"Yeah, maybe."

"Will there be a funeral?"

"Yeah, Ms. Bartlett is going to organize some kind of service. Mom can't deal with it herself."

"Well, those details are hard to deal with. Let me tell you a story. About a Yorkshireman whose wife died."

I took a biscuit and wondered if this Yorkshireman was really Mr. Adams.

He slurped some tea and smacked his lips. He rubbed his hands together, took an exaggerated breath and began.

"So, the Yorkshireman decides that his wife's headstone should 'ave the words *She were thine* engraved on it. He calls the stonemason, who assures him that the headstone will be ready a few days after the funeral. True to his word, the stonemason calls the widower to say that the headstone is ready and would he like to come and 'ave a look. When the widower gets there, he takes one look at the stone and sees that it's been engraved *She were thin.*

"He explodes. *Hells bells, man, you've left the bloody* e *out, you've left the bloody* e *out!*

"The stonemason apologizes profusely and assures the poor widower that it will be rectified the following mornin'. Next day comes and the widower returns to the stonemason. *There you go, sir, I've put the* e *on the stone for you.* The widower looks at the stone and then reads out aloud, *E, she were thin.*"

Then Mr. Adams screamed with laughter. He slapped the table and wiped tears from his eyes.

I stared at him.

"I thought you were going to tell me some deep, meaningful story."

"It's a joke, girl! A joke! To cheer you up."

I dropped my biscuit onto my plate. "Well, it's not particularly funny."

"Okay, how 'bout this one. A Yorkshireman with hemorrhoids on his bum asks the pharmacist, *Now then, lad, do you sell arse cream?* And the pharmacist replies, *Aye, chocolate or vanilla?*"

I burst out laughing. "Arse cream, ice cream. Good one, Mr. Adams."

"See? See? Bet that cheered you up, flower!"

I nodded and smiled. "Yep, that cheered me up."

I reached out and took his wrinkled hand. It was rough and cold, but it made me feel warm. How was that possible? I looked at the brown patches that covered his hand and knew that meant he was old. Nan had had those patches too. I hoped Mr. Adams lived a long, long time. I hoped he knew how much I cared.

He tried to pull away like he always did. He was probably thinking up some wisecrack. But I held his hand tight.

"Mr. Adams?"

His eyes were wide.

"I just want you to know that I'm really glad you're part of my life. You are very, very important to me."

He relaxed his arm and squeezed my hand.

"You're a crackin' lass, Kit. A right bobby dazzler."

I assumed it was a compliment and released my grip.

"Another cuppa?"

He nodded and started to get up.

"Sit your bum down, Mr. Adams," I said. "I'll get it."

Acknowledgments

Thanks:

- ~ To my two in-house teen critics: Duncan, for thinking out of the box, and Rosie, for her honesty.
- ~ To April, for playing independently when deadlines loomed.
- ~ To my siblings, for knowing things that I don't and sharing them with me.
- ~ To my mother, whose creativity inspires me, and to my father, who, truly, knows everything.
- ~ To the Schramp family, for being Mr. Adams's first fans.
- ~ To Kathy Stinson and Nan Forler, who gave criticism and encouragement equally, with no holds barred.
- ~ To Bob MacDonald, for writing "Gold in the Water" and allowing me to use his lyrics.
- ~ To all the writers and musicians who keep Newfoundland folk music alive. "Tickle Cove Pond" by Mark Walker and "The Petty Harbour Bait Skiff" by John Grace are but two examples of this vibrant tradition.
- ~ To my editor, Sarah Harvey, who made me a better writer with each stroke of her proverbial red pen.
- ~ Finally, to my husband, Robin Smith, for giving me the mantra "The laundry can wait."

Originally from Newfoundland, *Heather Smith* now lives in Waterloo, Ontario, with her husband and three children. Her Newfoundland roots inspire much of her writing. For more information, visit www.heathertsmith.com